THE CENTRAL LABORATORY

Max Jacob

THE CENTRAL LABORATORY

With a self-portrait by the author

Translated by Alexander Dickow

Wakefield Press

Cambridge, Massachusetts

Wakefield Press, P.O. Box 425645, Cambridge, MA 02142

Originally published in French as *Le laboratoire central* (Paris: Au sans pareil, 1921).

Some of these translations have previously appeared in the following journals: *Ekleksographia*, *Seedings*, and *Plume*.

This book was set in Minion Pro and Bernard MT Condensed by Wakefield Press. Printed and bound by McNaughton & Gunn, Inc., in the United States of America.

ISBN: 978-1-939663-80-1

Available through D.A.P./Distributed Art Publishers
75 Broad Street, Suite 630
New York, New York 10004
Tel: (212) 627-1999
Fax: (212) 627-9484

1   2   3   4   5   6   7   8   9   10

TABLE DES MATIÈRES

PREMIÈRE PARTIE

CONTENTS

SECOND PART

TROISIÈME PARTIE

DERNIÈRE PARTIE

LAST PART

1. POETRY IN VERSE

Max Jacob's extraordinary life has long overshadowed his work—to put it mildly. Best, then, to defer the biographical discussion and help the reader in appreciating a singularly perplexing body of work. Let's start with a few emblematic lines from "Incertitudes/Uncertainties" in its French and English versions:

> L'écrivain quelquefois sent le poids de l'azur
> Et puis d'avoir glissé sur la ruse du givre
> De tout l'hiver peut-être il n'aura le pain sûr.

> *In words the writer feels the azure weight*
> *And fallen on frost's ruse, that winter he*
> *Might not have bread all season on his plate.*

"The azure weight," in relation to the writer, is for those who frequent French poetry a transparent allusion to Mallarmé's poem "L'Azur," in which the poet obsesses over the deathless glare of the sky, which stands for the purity of an unattainable poetic ideal. Mallarmé ends the poem with a famous exclamation: "*Je suis hanté. L'azur! l'azur! l'azur! l'azur!*" ("*I am haunted.* The azure!" etc.—the reference to the color is most often rendered as "The sky! The sky! . . ." in English translation).

In French, the rhyming pair *azur* and *pain sûr*, literally "azure" and "bread for sure," strikes an astonishingly awkward note, for two reasons. First, the poet's unattainable ideal has taken quite a tumble from the sky and its divine ideal to the possibility of getting a bite to eat, mocking the bourgeois privilege that underpins Mallarmé's obsession. Mallarmé worries about lofty immaterial Ideas only because he has the leisure and material comfort to do so; in contrast, Jacob knew something of wretched poverty. But *azur/pain sûr* is also just a terrible rhyme: at best, forced; at worst, an affront to poets everywhere.

At this point, some readers might abandon the book and decide that the poet's mastery is deficient. They would be wrong, although Jacob, with his customary humility, does self-identify as a perpetual "novice in art," as he says in "Perigal-Nohor." All signs point to a voluntary gesture in "Uncertainties": for the poet has "fallen" on the (once again very Mallarméan) "frost," and that pratfall leads directly into the poetic nosedive with which the poem concludes. (In this respect, my translation has failed; "weight" and "plate" are perfectly acceptable rhymes: I tried to compensate for this unfortunate rhyming success with an awkward enjambment in the previous line, "that winter he / Might not have . . .")

The Central Laboratory was published in 1921, shortly before the official end of Parisian Dadaism in 1922, by the publisher Au Sans Pareil (the original edition features a self-portrait by Jacob as a frontispiece, included here). To some extent, Jacob's poetry partakes of the spirit of Dadaism, albeit with a much greater dose of existential affirmation and considerably less angst. For what makes Max Jacob so surprising—so downright *jarring*—to read is precisely the way he manages to defy readerly expectations at their most fundamental level, where it really hurts.

Many poets, particularly among avant-gardes of the 1910s and '20s in Paris, claim to defy expectations. But how genuinely shocking are their provocations? They produced a great deal more charm or hilarity than outrage, and the tumult at the premiers of *Rite of Spring* or *Parade* was largely staged or overstated. Jacob understood that shock means radically destabilizing canons of taste, which is why some moments in his poetry read like weirdly cockeyed doggerel, that poetic crime of crimes within the practice of formal verse. In other words, those moments—mixed in with verses of incredible grace, refinement, and delicacy whose arrival is just as unexpected— are very much designed to be doggerel, and to offend the ear of the aesthete. Looking for poetic harmonies? You might be disappointed (although more on that anon). In fact, in the 1920s, Jacob framed his poetics precisely in terms of "disappointment": "Read *The Dice Cup*! A story was started and left unfinished, the reader was slid from place to place until there was nothing left [. . .]. The art of disappointment [*déception*] was that of *glissando*, of stupefying others, of gratuitousness, of frivolity."[1] The word in French for disappointment is *déception*, but its etymology comes from the same meaning as the English *deception*, and Jacob seems to have the etymology, and perhaps the English cognate, very much in mind. For this art of "disappointment" is precisely the art of sabotaging readers' expectations, of producing doubt and disorientation, perhaps even sadness or a slight sense of having been jilted.

The Dice Cup is well known for these kinds of effects (or at least much more so than Jacob's verse poems), as in "Poem" ("When our ship reached . . ."):

When our ship reached the Indian Ocean islands, we realized we had no maps. We had to disembark! It was then we discovered who was on board: that bloodthirsty man who gives his wife tobacco, only to snatch it back. The islands were scattered everywhere. On the cliff-top, we could make out some little black men in bowler hats. "Maybe they'll have some maps." We took the cliff path: it was a rope ladder; perhaps along the ladder there would be some maps, maybe even Japanese maps. We kept going up. Finally, when there were no more rungs (ivory crabs in some places), we had to climb using our wrists. My African brother acquitted himself very well, while I discovered some rungs where there hadn't been any. Having reached the top, we're on a wall. My brother leaps off. Me, I'm at the window. I could never make up my mind to jump: it's a wall made of red boards: "Walk around it," my African brother cries out. There are no more steps, nor passengers, nor boat, nor little black man; there's the tour still to be done. But what tour? It's disheartening.[2]

The lost traveler—who never reaches his destination, naturally—is a motif emblematic of anxious dreams and Jacob's poetry alike, and Jacob commented at length on the seeming unreality of scenarios like these as early as 1907, in a letter to an editor who may have been the Polish emigré Mécislas Golberg:

It has been recommended that artists use *surprise* (I'm starting in on the psychological issue): but that is the wrong word. Surprise is a stable state. The old psychologists used to say, rightly according to me, that pleasure is in movement; the spectator must be *tossed to and fro*; aesthetic emotion is doubt. Doubt is obtainable through the coupling of that which is incompatible (and without producing stable surprise), by the harmony of different languages, by the complexity of temperaments: showing the man in the hero, the virtue in vice as in Racine and Molière: in poetry, interest is born of doubt between reality and the imagination, the perturbation of epochs and in positive habits. Music and painting have no other law. Doubt, that is art![3]

In the preceding prose poem, the hesitation between "reality and the imagination" pervades the text, so that the reader identifies with the poet's disorientation. This "doubt" as a fundamental poetic principle prefigures the "art of disappointment" proposed by Jacob close to twenty years later, and both of these theoretical discussions are broadly applicable to his prose poetry in *The Dice Cup*. Jacob is also anticipating, in this very early letter, the crisis in the very concept of the work of art that cubism and Dada would soon explore (if doubt is art, does art even exist as such?). In addition to the prose poem, the art of disappointment (or deception?)—along with doubt, naturally—also plays a huge role in Jacob's verse poetry of the modernist period; that is, roughly until 1927's *Fond de l'eau*, when his poetry takes a somewhat different turn, though it never entirely abandons the vertiginous ironies and acrobatics of the 1910s and early '20s (in particular, the notion of "emotion" and interiority would become more and more crucial to Jacob's conception of poetry, at the expense of technical and formal considerations). In his verse poems, narrative—incomplete or otherwise—is sometimes negligible, while versification becomes crucial, as our initial example suggests. Rhyme schemes and meter are engines of readerly expectation; the reader waits for one rhyme to answer the previous one. Jacob cannot resist any sort of verbal machine, certainly not this one. He plays relentlessly with meter and rhyme, introducing awkward caesurae that slice through words, exceeding or cutting short the all-too-standard twelve-syllable French alexandrine line.

Only Verlaine and Apollinaire, perhaps, blended traditional and free-verse forms with as much plasticity as Jacob (in fact, had Jacob published his verse poems earlier, such as in 1903 when some of these poems were written, he might have received more credit for his experiments). Not making an honorable attempt at translating Jacob's versification seemed to me to risk neglecting a major dimension of his art:

> Posthumous ball in costume
> Where the crowd is inflamed for not having lanced its
>   imposthume ("The Masked Ball")

Here, Jacob explodes the bounds of the alexandrine in order to exemplify the idea of the "imposthume," a painful, swollen abscess: all the while, rhymes in -*ume* proliferate like an obsession (abscession?).

I was not always able to mimic every dimension of Jacob's verse technique. One characteristic I found myself unable to replicate faithfully is Jacob's aversion to enjambment. The poet seems to have taken to heart Stéphane Mallarmé's description of what a line of verse should be; namely, that the line should "make a new and total word" out of "several vocables" (from his famous essay "Crise de vers"). If Jacob's verse poetry has a standard unit, it is the line, a unit I sometimes found myself forced to break open, usually to maintain a difficult rhyme. Hopefully, I have mostly avoided this pitfall, and maintained the line-by-line feel of Jacob's versification.

Let me say more about this line-by-line feel. In French criticism, for close to a century now, the term *coq-à-l'âne* often appears in discussions of Max Jacob's verse style. The term, which literally means *from the cock to the donkey*, refers to a form of cryptic "nonsense" verse whose extreme thematic disjunction disguises some kind of satirical commentary. One might describe *coq-à-l'âne* verse as "jumping from apples to oranges." A relative of the *fatrasies* of the Middle Ages—closer to true nonsense verse—and to incantatory formulae, the *coq-à-l'âne*'s most important practitioner was the Renaissance poet Clément Marot. Arguably, Max Jacob is its most effective modern practitioner, such as in the enigmatic "Léon! Léon!":

The hay in the woods the noise of footsteps
My fat cousin in a bedroom
Explain it to me! Explain it to me!
I don't have the courage to put on the other slipper.

There are few sonic effects to justify the disjunctions; they approach the form of Apollinaire's famous conversation-poems, such as "Lundi rue Christine," which appears to incorporate fragments of overheard conversation on the busy street of the same name. This is modernist experimentation at its most obvious. But much more often, Jacob's verses do in fact have strong thematic connections, and even evolve in quasi-narrative fashion. The disjunction, often syntactic in nature, is here much more subtle and elusive:

> And yet! three flowers . . . three sobs!
> Bundle, off with you! There's still the monument
> Epitaph, speeches so eloquent. ("Meditation on Death")

The thematic connection to death is transparent here, but the poet maintains the sense of a leap, or jump, or slight disconnection between the lines. Jacob's often unconventional punctuation, notably his tendency to continue sentences beyond exclamation and question marks through the use of lower case, such as in the first line of "Let us! sing the whale . . . ," certainly contributes to this sense of slight discontinuity. The absence of periods leads one to believe that the proposition is about to continue, which it fails to do (once again, the art of deception or disappointment): "There's still the monument / Epitaph, speeches so eloquent." The relationship of these two lines is purely appositional; there is no syntax relating the words into the structure of a sentence, even though there's an evident logical connection between epitaphs and monuments. The *feeling* of apples-to-oranges is maintained even where there is conceptual continuity.

Many of Jacob's other poems rely not on thematic or formal disjunction, but on the transformational continuities of sonic play. The presence of puns or pun-like verbal associations is a constant of Jacob's poetry, in prose and verse poems alike. The pun, as Jonathan Culler has observed in *On Puns*, is the most déclassé of rhetorical figures, but for Jacob, it is also fundamental to the act of poetic creation, allowing the writer to bounce from one sonority to the next, from one word to its neighbor.[4] Rhyme bears an essential kinship with the pun, and Jacob once referred to rhymes as "half-puns";[5] hence Jacob's enjoyment of particularly strange rhyming pairs (rare or regional terms, proper names, or foreign words, for instance).

Jacob's interest in rare words, and especially in proper names of all kinds, goes hand in hand with his interest in paronomasia and punning; proper names (and unfamiliar terms also) can be readily exploited for the latent meanings suggested by their sound. The word *nom* ("name") is already in "Agamemnon," as the rhyme in "Concerning Several Invitations" suggests. In his preface to the Gallimard edition of *The Central Laboratory*, the philosopher Yvon Belaval, who knew the poet, discusses the collection as a kind of combination bestiary-herbarium, brimming with proper names of plants and animals—among them, the wonderfully diverse varieties of human being real and imaginary, from the Duke of Otranto to the eighteenth-century poet Jacques Clinchamps de Malfilâtre. Many of these names will be unfamiliar to most Americans, and I have added notes where they can assist in understanding the poems, but it is also worthwhile to yield to their mystery, as Jacob probably intended.

Eliminating these kinds of effects, including rhyme, proper names, or meter, would only deface Jacob's careful edifice, and spoil a great deal of the fun. The same goes for any number of poems in *The Central Laboratory*, especially delightful near-nonsense poems like "Acidulous Music" or "War and Peace," which rely heavily on meter, rhyme, and sound to exert their peculiar charm ("War and Peace" is surely among the oddest of nonsense poems).

Jacob's play with versification might explain why *The Central Laboratory*'s fate has been so different from that of his book of prose poems, *The Dice Cup*, published just four years earlier, in 1917. *The Dice Cup* left a deep mark on French poetry and its readers, particularly through future surrealists like Louis Aragon and Philippe Soupault (and even André Breton, though the homophobic, antireligious "pope" of surrealism would soon dismiss Jacob as an influence), as well as on young poets less well-known in the United States, such as Louis Émié. But Jacob's reputation in the 1920s and '30s rested not on the prose poems but on the poems in verse. Surveys, literary histories, and anthologies of the period draw from the verse poems in preference to the prose poems. Nowadays, *The Dice Cup* is probably Jacob's only truly canonical work, as misunderstood as it remains (there's a dearth of maps, you see). Why have these two works changed places? Probably in part because readers today are less sensitive to the complexities of versification. One must know the rules of counterpoint to understand the proper depth of Mozart's "A Musical Joke," and the same goes for Max Jacob's verse poems.

Compare Jacob's absurdity with that of Soupault and Breton's *Magnetic Fields*, or Breton's *Soluble Fish*, or Benjamin Péret's *Grand Jeu*. Readers have no problem with the nonsensical or fantastical elements of such works. They do not complain that these poets are "disconcerting" (as Gide says of Jacob),[6] because all of these works adopt total formal freedom, dispensing with all traces of traditional forms. Jacob never does so. He seems to send us mixed signals, making us search in vain for rationales that do not always exist, overarching messages where signification may remain sparse and local. We assume that where there is structure there is meaning-making, but Jacob's absurdity and propensity for arbitrary verbal play is as prominent as that of any surrealist, although meaning sometimes flashes through much of what first appeared purely random. In fact, the only truly surrealist text in *The Central Laboratory* might be "Death," a short word-salad whose title may suggest that the poem is designed to show the fruitlessness and sterility of surrealist automatic writing or Dadaist word-music. Unlike the experience of reading such indifferent piles of words, Jacob's poems reward *persistence*. As the poet wrote, "I would like you to read it not for a long time, but to read it often: to be understood leads to being loved."[7]

Here are a few particularly obvious examples of doubt, deception, and disappointment in the poems of *The Central Laboratory*, ones that take place not between one line and the next, as is the case with rhyme and meter, but at the scale of entire poems, where these slippery tricks may be more obvious. This poem, for instance, begins joyfully:

What fine downstrokes written by the sea! No doubt
No doubt forever, forever blotted out,
Just a word and we'll be off again
We'll be off, baroom! to rack our brain—

The "downstrokes" are those of writing, a jubilant exercise here, leading to an onomatopoeic outburst or verbal explosion, "baroom!" but also an eternally futile exercise, as the sea's down-strokes are "forever blotted out." The poet announces a new departure upon the waves: "Just a word and we'll be off again / [...] to rack our brain," but the voyage is already metaphorical, a voyage into the vagaries of thought. And racking one's brain is no longer quite so jubilant. Indeed, the tone turns quite quickly in a darker direction, and soon enough, we have our imaginary sailors eating overcooked seagull, "dry as leather." "Even so does my mind, etc." concludes the poem very abruptly.

What to make of this sudden abbreviation? We already know, in fact, since the journey is framed as "racking" the poet's brain, that we are witness to an allegory for a journey of the imagination. In a Baudelairian allegory like "The Giant" or "The Albatross," the poem would inevitably explain some of the metaphors in explicit terms, showing how the concrete corresponds to various abstract concepts. Late medieval allegorical Arthurian legend operates in much the same way: after an episode is recounted, the narrator offers the "senefiance" or true meaning of each narrative emblem.

Jacob's refusal to provide the "true meanings" and conceptual correspondences serves a double purpose. On the one hand, it mocks allegory as a laborious exercise that infantilizes the reader. That reader might indeed explain for herself what the concrete elements of this poem might signify. For instance, the hard, unyielding flesh of the seagull might suggest the resistance of the object of thought, its intractability (a universal experience, perhaps, for those who have written papers on literature with any frequency). Second, the poet echoes the erasure of writing with which the poem began: like the sea, the poem's conclusion has been wiped away by the successive waves of thought. *On y pense, on oublie*: in one ear and out the other. The poem has elaborated a paradoxical, subverted allegory that, while still operating as allegory, refuses to fulfill the promise intrinsic to the form. This might serve as a paradigm for Jacob's "art of disappointment": the poem gives with one hand what it takes away with the other.

"To M. Modigliani to Prove to Him I Am a Poet" performs a similar subversion of the poet's vocational scenario, a rather humble version of the mythology of romantic genius:

> As a child I was gifted and the sky
> Would then parade my charming reverie
> Eclipsing pennants of reality.
> In the middle my friends to angels nigh,
> I knew not who I was, and wrote a bit.

But this poem's main interest is in its overall movement and sudden shifts in tone, and this vocational scenario suddenly swerves toward Jacob's religious preoccupations: toward his encounter with God.

The poem begins with a series of alexandrines (which I've rendered, as I generally do in this collection, in English pentameter), but these begin to give way to tetrameter (octosyllables in the French), sustained through the rest of the poem until the last two lines, which abandon both rhyme and meter entirely. This is analogous to finishing a song by allowing it to suddenly fall apart in a random clatter of sound, a stylistic tic of 1990s indie rock bands. But in Jacob's poem, the formal collapse dramatizes the "demons" who come to "cave in the cloud," to corrupt the poem's formal perfection. The clouds had been, in the beginning of the poem, the object of the poet's contemplation, a heavenly contemplation that itself served as a sign of poetic (and divine) election. To cave them in is to shatter the vision of divine harmony the poet pretends to reveal; it is also a very deliberate artistic pratfall much akin to the clunky "azure/ bread for sure" finale of "Uncertainties" analyzed above. Once again, the poet resists closure in favor of a gesture ambiguous to those who pay close attention to metrical form.

I've been stressing the radicality of Jacob's poetics, his ability to destabilize the reader, his weird juxtaposition of wildly different codes—I've been situating Jacob's verse poems as an alternative avant-garde paralleling that of the surrealists, his contemporaries. Still to account for is Jacob's debt to Romantic poets like Alfred de Musset or Lord Byron (both of whom he read extensively as a young man), and more generally, the sentimental depth of feeling Jacob's work often exhibits. "Le Départ/ The Departure" demonstrates Jacob's ability to slip into high lyricism. The melancholic repetition of the word "farewell" prefigures Margaret Wise Brown's *Goodnight Moon*, whose refrain of goodbyes has marked so many childhoods. Certainly, there are touches of Jacob's signature weirdness in the unexpectedly "oval" river and the slightly comical farewell to the very prosaic "laundry." But the piece's emotional force is real, and appears elsewhere too (e.g., "The Screamer," "Villonelle"). This sometimes has an old-fashioned air, as though Jacob were indeed hearkening back to a much older kind of poetry, but once again, it's Jacob's *mixed messages*, his wild veering between different poetic languages, that make him so hard to pin down. "The Departure" is full of a delicate melancholy. It's an exquisitely refined poem (one which the American poet Ron Padgett has closely imitated in "Homage to Max Jacob"), but it precedes the incongruous moralizing and poetic pratfalls of "Uncertainties" (the azure again!). The reader, as the French would say, doesn't know which foot to dance on. Perhaps the same foot as Jacob's delightful citrus fruit: "The dancer:—a lemon zest— / Pursues Diana, hide-and-seek . . ." In any event, whether you choose the left or the right foot, you can't go wrong with a good Sardana:

> The people were like the waves of the seas
> If the seas were a spinning rose at night
> If the night were rose, if rose were the seas
> And if the seas themselves were like green trees.

2. THE LIFE

"Honor of the Sardana and the Tenora" is dedicated to Picasso, and it introduces us to one of Jacob's critical relationships.

As Jacob's biographer Rosanna Warren recently suggested, he had the ambiguous fortune of being surrounded by a number of very great individuals, and his posthumous reputation has been unjustly obscured by their long shadows.[8] Jacob met Picasso in 1901 and became the glorious painter's friend in his early years in Paris, bearing witness to the birth of cubism and to the painter's growing fame. During those years, both Jacob and Picasso grew close to Guillaume Apollinaire—it was in fact Picasso who introduced them in 1904, at a bar called Austin's Fox. For a number of years, Jacob lived at 7 rue Ravignan, a few doors down from the famous Bateau-Lavoir, an architectural curiosity where Picasso and many other artists made their more or less temporary home over the years. The rue Ravignan became a place of legend, and it gave its name to Jacob's "The Rue Ravignan."

But Jacob's story is much more than that of Apollinaire and Picasso's close friend. That story began twenty-five years before he met Picasso, in Quimper, Brittany, the poet's birthplace and hometown, which for him was endowed with a permanent ache of nostalgia—see, for instance, "The Departure" and "A Thousand Regrets" ("Mille regrets"). In the early 1920s he completed a vast satirical fresco of Quimper in his novel *Le Terrain Bouchaballe* (The Bouchaballe Lot).[9] Late in the decade he invented a heteronym, Morven le Gaélique, poet of Breton songs. Brittany was a permanent fixture of his imagination. Some have suggested that *The Central Laboratory* wages a kind of battle between rue Ravignan and Quimper, between the poet's lost Garden and his adoptive home in Paris.

Jacob was born into a family of prosperous shop owners on 12 July 1876 (the poet often claimed he was born on the more astrologically propitious 11th). They were a nonpracticing Jewish family, and Jacob's relationship with Judaism is still a subject of some debate. But the shadow of Quimper's granite cathedral loomed over the poet's destiny. In 1909, Jacob experienced a mystical vision, an angel or Christ-like figure inhabiting a landscape, displayed and moving across a wall of his room on rue Ravignan. Jacob was already fascinated by religious thought (particularly the syncretic imagination of turn-of-the-century theosophy); over time, however, he was drawn increasingly to Catholicism. He converted and was baptized in 1915, with Picasso as his godfather.

In 1921, shortly after the publication of *The Central Laboratory*, Jacob withdrew from Paris to the small town of Saint-Benoît-sur-Loire, site of a seventh-century abbey. In the wake of the Great War and the Spanish flu, Paris was a difficult place in which to survive, rife with shortages, a situation that no doubt influenced Jacob's decision to leave the city at such an inopportune time for his literary career, just when his collection was released and needed promotion. Jacob would live in Saint Benoît until 1928, when he moved back to Paris in an attempt (thwarted in the end by various life circumstances) to relaunch his career as a writer and painter. He then returned again to Saint-Benoît in 1936, where he remained until 1944, publishing little, especially after 1938, when Jews were forbidden to publish under Vichy law. There he lived a quiet and ardently religious life, subsisting mostly thanks to his painting. He was a lifelong painter, though that aspect of his work is less celebrated than his writing. A gallery of Quimper's museum is dedicated to his paintings. Jacob was arrested by the Gestapo in 1944 and sent to the Drancy concentration camp, a last stop before transport to Auschwitz, but he died of pneumonia before he could be deported, on 5 March, only a little more than a week after his arrest in Saint-Benoît. There have been many rumors of an order being issued to liberate Jacob: no such order has been found, and it's unlikely that this liberation ever existed. Likewise, legend has it that Picasso, Cocteau, and others were guilty of doing little to save Jacob, but the reality is that they mostly did what they could, which was very little.[10]

It's impossible to overstate the importance of Catholicism and the doctrines of the church to Jacob. He was no saint, but he aspired to holiness, and he was far from lukewarm in his piety; he practiced prayer and written meditation daily, went to mass systematically; he took theology and religious dogma very seriously. He had a particular terror of Hell, which his meditations often evoke in detail. In particular, he felt deep guilt and self-loathing with regard to his homosexuality, but more generally with regard to physical pleasures such as drinking and effusive displays of sentiment, and he identified strongly with the ascetic ideal of detachment from earthly delights in the search for the forgiveness of sin. His poetry pervasively evokes the issue of homosexuality, at times subtly, offering the occasional confession:

> Farewell, muse, go tell the men
> While the party's on again
> That in prisons where we lie
> For having loved them, we die.
> ("Plaintes d'un prisonnier/A Prisoner's Complaints")

His homosexuality played a major role in his life. His attitude toward his sexuality is expressed in the plainest terms in a letter to Louis Émié, who was also homosexual.

> No! no! forget him! forget the others! take refuge in marriage, in piety, in work, and never forget, in the middle of Bordeaux's cynicism, that we are monsters the heavens abhor, that the world abhors, that we are accursed. If you knew what looks I've come across in my life, what silences. Don't you believe that Gide or Cocteau would have a status *that they don't have* and will never have.[11]

"Accursed." This belief explains why Max Jacob does not play quite the role of LGBTQIA+ icon or role model that, say, Claude Cahun or Hervé Guibert might be said to (although these remarks to Émié need to be placed in context: beyond his undeniable personal shame, Jacob is concerned that his young provincial friend will be condemned to a life of secrecy in order to lead a successful literary career). Indeed, Jacob cannot act as unequivocal role model or poster boy for any particular identity: he is too full of contrasts and contradictions for that. Nonetheless, Jacob was very much a part of the homosexual social circles of the 1920s and '30s, as Rosanna Warren shows in her biography. He knew Gide and Cocteau, and high-powered socialites like François de Gouy d'Arcy and Russell Greeley, as well as Natalie Clifford Barney, Marsden Hartley, and many other figures of that period.

Poet, painter, Catholic convert, Jewish, Breton, dandy, bohemian, gay man, astrologist, clown, mystic, ironist, post-Romantic sentimentalist—that's a lot of costumes to wear. And the poetry—and his fiction, too—overflows with colorful masks. One mode of such masking is pastiche and parody, those textual techniques that allow Jacob to caricature other writers. Titles indicate many other identities: in "Le Départ du marin/The Seaman's Departure," the poet imagines himself as a sailor, and as an explorer in "L'Explorateur/The Explorer." Elsewhere the persona is implicit: in "Madame X . . . ," he imagines himself a lady's man scolding a flirt. In "As a Family," it's as the eldest son in a large bourgeois family, though Jacob was not the eldest in his own. The list goes on.

The series "Characters from a Masked Ball" is well known in France thanks to Francis Poulenc's *Bal Masqué*, based on several poems from this suite. Portraits of third-person characters rather than personae adopted by the poet himself, they nonetheless involve the same play of appearances (and the same satirical spirit that is central to Jacob's poetics). Jacob's worldview everywhere displays Plato's dichotomy between appearance and reality—but there may be layer upon layer of appearance, like an onion, as he explained half-facetiously to Apollinaire.[12] God is the only ultimate reality. Jacob is a poet of *Schein*, as Schiller conceived it: the capacity for illusion that allows human beings to play. And Jacob plays even when the stakes could hardly be more serious.

The carnival atmosphere of *The Central Laboratory* seems appropriate to the sumptuous 1920s, the age of the Bœuf sur le toit cabaret, of the discovery of jazz in France, of *Les Six* and Ravel, of so many marvels of modern culture. In reality, the collection's poems span more than seventeen years—from 1903, when the earliest were written, to 1920 or 1921. Originally, Jacob may have projected a collection called *Christ in Montparnasse*, which he seems to have later divided into *The Central Laboratory* and 1919's *Defense of Tartufe*.[13] While *The Central Laboratory* by no means lacks religious content, it is more formally experimental and diverse than the *Defense*, even in the overtly Catholic poems. The *Defense*, which tends to be more restrained and discursive, foregrounds the author's life and his conversion, recounting events in prose and verse in various genres, while *The Central Laboratory* showcases the poet's formal innovation, his satirical verve, and his indulgence in the aforementioned characters and masks.

3. MAX JACOB IN THE UNITED STATES

Interest in Max Jacob in English begins with S. J. Collier's mostly biographical dissertation.[14] In 1957, Collier published what was to prove the first of many articles devoted to a text often considered Jacob's major statement on the poetics of the prose poem, the 1916 preface to *The Dice Cup*.[15] The 1915 controversy between Jacob and his one-time mentee Pierre Reverdy made for a fertile field of investigation, and since Collier's time, some half-dozen scholarly articles have focused on this preface. With its theoretical apparatus thus in full view, *The Dice Cup* itself became an object of study, particularly by way of its prominent use of intertextual techniques including pastiche, parody, and all their relatives. Sydney Lévy in particular focused on these procedures.[16] But Lévy, inspired at the time by structuralism, makes of Jacob a kind of proto-Oulipian formalist, a creator of essentially gratuitous verbal machines, unconcerned with the moral or social dimension of writing.[17]

The Dice Cup is indeed Jacob's least overtly religious work, and can sustain this kind of formal analysis. But as even a cursory reader of *The Central Laboratory* must realize, Jacob is formalist only to the extent that he cares to disturb the serene surface of the poem in order to innovate and disrupt. Beyond that point, he remains a Catholic satirist eminently concerned with social mores, particularly among the French bourgeoisie he despised (and from which he came). Poems like "La Marâtre moderne/The Modern Wicked Stepmother," though tinged with a dated misogyny common in the satirical tradition,[18] can hardly be read outside of a moralistic frame, whatever their various weird poetic devices. The same goes for "Slumber! sun!

take up the blinds . . . ," a celebration of the sanctity of marriage, which the gay bachelor Jacob often praised as a social good. The satirists to which Jacob owes his greatest debt are no doubt the authors of opérettes and opera-bouffes of the nineteenth century, particularly Hervé and Offenbach, in whose deceptively lighthearted verses and music the author had been soaked from a young age; the music-halls and cabarets of 1890s France are not far behind (think Alphonse Allais, Aristide Bruant, the Chat Noir, and the like). In Jacob's avant-garde poetry, there is still quite a bit of Offenbach's *Orpheus in the Underworld*, an ingredient that only adds to the confusion of poetic codes at play in *The Central Laboratory*.

Unfortunately, Jacob's critical reception in the United States has not advanced far beyond the formalist approaches of the 1970s. It is instead among contemporary poets that Jacob's legacy has been maintained and prolonged, through influential translations and translators (John Ashbery among them), admirers who advertise their debt to Jacob, as Stephen Dunn does in his prose poem collection *Reciprocities*, and as Ian Seed and John Fuller do in the UK. Seed will be releasing a new translation of *The Dice Cup*, and Fuller has named a recent collection of his own *Dice Cup* in homage to Jacob. The poet Mark Weiss is a longtime admirer of Jacob's work, and has published translations of his prose poems. Sampson Starkweather, cofounder of the successful poetry press Birds, LLC, has written brilliant pastiches of Jacob's prose poems. Jacob is almost a modest iconic figure of contemporary American poetry, alongside Francis Ponge and Henri Michaux.

Nonetheless, only one full-length translation of Jacob's *Dice Cup* existed before Ian Seed's translation for Wakefield

Press (self-published by its translator, Michael Rosenthal, in 2019). Christopher Pilling and David Kennedy published half of the volume for Atlas Press in 2000, and several selected collections existed before that, including translations by Ashbery and David Ball in a volume edited by Michael Brownstein in 1979. Paul Auster, another notable admirer of Jacob's work, included a selection of his poems in his celebrated *Random House Anthology of 20th-Century French Poetry*, while Andrei Codrescu, another singular character and editor of the journal *Exquisite Corpse*, also translated Jacob (*For Max Jacob*, Tree Books, 1974). William Kulik has published a selected volume of prose poems by Jacob (*Selected Poems of Max Jacob*, Oberlin College Press, 1999), and another selection in *Dreaming the Miracle: Three French Prose Poets* (White Pine Press, 2002). Everywhere the prose poem has dominated, with the sole exception of Maria Green and Moishe Black's anthology of excerpts from Jacob's other prose works, *Hesitant Fire* (University of Nebraska Press, 1991). The problem with all these volumes, besides the outsized influence of the prose poetry, is their scattershot or piecemeal approach (why publish *half* of a book?). For a poet so easily misunderstood and so against the grain of convention, this is particularly unfortunate. We've been looking through a keyhole at a cathedral. It is to be hoped that Wakefield's dual publication of the entire *Dice Cup* and *The Central Laboratory*, along with Rosanna Warren's recent English-language biography, will do something to broaden perspectives, and perhaps encourage further translation of Jacob's work.

Is this already something of a comeback for Jacob's work? The poet's reception in France remains ambiguous: university scholarship largely ignores Jacob and thinks of him as a distinctly unserious writer, but a small contingent of dedicated scholars have, against this current, reignited interest in the poet by way of a specialized journal, the *Cahiers Max Jacob* (2006–present), an omnibus anthology assembling most of the poet's most important work (*Œuvres*, 2012, edited by Antonio Rodriguez with a biographical introduction by Rodriguez and Patricia Sustrac), a biography by Béatrice Mousli (2004), and a *Dictionnaire Max Jacob* forthcoming in 2024 with entries from more than seventy contributors. If this critical renaissance has so far somewhat escaped the attention of the French critical establishment, in the long run, Jacob has become a more or less permanent part of the literary landscape, alongside Apollinaire, Blaise Cendrars, or Pierre Reverdy.

But Jacob's contribution to that landscape remains unique; he is ultimately *sui generis*. His poetics put into practice recent ideas about "queering" literary style—how else to describe the "art of disappointment" and the poetics of "doubt" if not in terms of strategies of resistance to *normalizing* reading and understanding texts and identities? The same analogy can be drawn between Jacob's poetics and the idea of "camp," an aesthetic that challenges notions of value and taste; Jacob's engagement with popular genres—operettas and opera-bouffe, but also Breton folksongs, nonsense poetry, nursery rhymes, weirdly contorted doggerel, pastiche and parody, and just plain puns—all participate in the joyous, carnivalesque confusion of high and low culture in Jacob's poetry. These analogies suggest just how timely Jacob's poetry remains, and it perhaps helps to explain why Jacob has remained a force in American poetry, in which the likes of Frank O'Hara, Jack Spicer, and Gertrude

Stein loom very large. Jacob is very much a part of that poetic family.

An introduction always hopes to dispel readers' potential resistance, to commit them entirely to the work at hand—in short, to seduce them. But this particular introduction might be better called an *avertissement*, a *caution* to readers not to trust first impressions and easy assumptions too readily, to allow for the truly unexpected, to look beyond the clown into the eyes of the mystic. Those willing to look closely will find their poetic reward. Read often and reflect: to understand this work is to love it.

NOTES

1. Robert Guiette, *La Vie de Max Jacob* (Paris: Nizet, 1976), 130–131. This volume was published in its entirety in 1976, but the interviews on which it is based were conducted with the poet in the 1920s.

2. Max Jacob, *The Dice Cup*, translated by Ian Seed (Cambridge, MA: Wakefield Press, forthcomin in 2022).

3. Max Jacob, *Œuvres* (Paris: Gallimard, 2012), 163–164, my translation.

4. Jonathan Culler, *On Puns: The Foundation of Letters* (Oxford: Blackwell, 1988), 6.

5. Max Jacob, *Œuvres*, 1702.

6. From a text written in 1927 collected in André Gide, *Essais critiques* (Paris: Gallimard, 1999), 912.

7. Jacob, *The Dice Cup*, forthcoming.

8. Rosanna Warren, *Max Jacob: A Life in Art and Letters* (New York: W. W. Norton, 2020).

9. An excerpt of this novel appears in *Hesitant Fire*, Moishe Black and Maria Green's selection of translated excerpts of Jacob's prose works (Lincoln: University of Nebraska Press, 1991).

10. On Max Jacob's arrest and subsequent final days, see Patricia Sustrac's crucial article "La Mort de Max Jacob: réalité et representations," *Cahiers Max Jacob*, no. 9 (2009): 103–118. Alongside Béatrice Mousli and Rosanna Warren, authors of Jacob's most complete biographies, Patricia Sustrac's biographical, historical, and bibliophilic research on Jacob has been instrumental in renewing research on the poet. The present translation owes something to Sustrac's tireless work and steadfast friendship, as does all my work on Max Jacob.

11. Unpublished correspondence, letter of 15 July 1926, my translation. The last sentence suggests that Gide and Cocteau would have had an even greater glory were they not homosexual: in hindsight, the comment seems misplaced, given the stature of these two figures.

12. See Jacob, *Œuvres*, 165–166.

13. A "Tartufe" is any generic religious hypocrite, while Tartuffe with two f's designates Molière's famous character. A manuscript with the title *Le Christ a Montparnasse* was given to the collector Jacques Doucet, in whose collection it remains; the manuscript includes many poems from both collections. However, it's unclear whether Jacob intended to publish these poems together; he may have assembled the manuscript specifically to gratify the collector's desire for a manuscript, rather than in view of a publication in any similar form.

14. S. J. Collier, "Max Jacob, le poète pénitent de Saint-Benoît," PhD dissertation, University of Leeds, 1950.

15. "Max Jacob's *Cornet à dés*: A Critical Analysis," *French Studies* 11, no. 2 (April 1957): 149–167.

16. Sydney Lévy, *The Play of the Text: Max Jacob's* Cornet à dés (Madison: University of Wisconsin Press, 1981).

17. Not all studies reduced Jacob to formalism, however; note the study by Judith Morganroth Schneider, *Clown at the Altar: The Religious Poetry of Max Jacob* (Chapel Hill: University of North Carolina Press, 1978). However, this study barely involves his prose poetry, focusing instead on Jacob's verse poems.

18. To cover the chapter of women in Max Jacob's work would demand another preface entirely, but two things may be noted: first, Jacob's relationship to his mother, with whom he also identified strongly, was tense and ambivalent; second, Jacob sometimes identified his own homosexuality metaphorically with femininity, and as such, his misogyny is in part a function of his own self-loathing, since he

experienced deep guilt about his sexuality. This does not excuse the misogyny, which is an unfortunate feature of his work.

PREMIÈRE PARTIE

FIRST PART

À Georges Auric

Il se peut qu'un rêve étrange
Vous ait occupée ce soir,
Vous avez cru voir un ange
Et c'était votre miroir.

Dans sa fuite Éléonore
A défait ses longs cheveux
Pour dérober à l'aurore
Le doux objet de mes vœux.

À quelque mari fidèle
Il ne faudra plus penser.
Je suis amant, j'ai des ailes
Je vous apprends à voler.

Que la muse du mensonge
Apporte au bout de vos doigts
Ce dédain qui n'est qu'un songe
Du berger plus fier qu'un roi.

For Georges Auric[1]

PERHAPS the strangest of dreams
     Was on your mind tonight, for
You saw an angel, it seems
And yet it was your mirror.

When Eleanor took flight
She let down all her tresses
To steal from morning light
The object of my wishes.

There's no use in believing
In any faithful husband.
I teach flying, I take wing
I'm on a lover's errand.

Let the muse of lies bring
your fingertips disdain
A fancy just as vain
As shepherds proud as kings.

Honneur de la sardane et de la tenora ▃▃▃▃

Dédié à Picasso

MER est la mer Égée qui dépasse Alicante.
Ah! que n'ai-je vingt-cinq mille livres de rentes!
Les montagnes veillaient sur la mer et la ville.
Sur les murs s'étalait le blason de Castille;
Des églises carrées et les maisons aussi
Et les gens ont toujours l'air de vous dire merci.
Tous ces Romains seraient de l'Opéra-Comique
Si la toge jamais pouvait être comique.
Bleu de cravates bleues aux forains dépassant.
Si les pruneaux étaient couleur d'olive claire
Ce seraient des pruneaux que ces vieillards sévères,
Ces vieillards sont trop maigres; trop gros ces jeunes gens!
Les gitanes iront au cinématographe
Les chevreaux futures outres ont des cous de girafes
Des Catalans phrygiens vendaient des escargots
Les tartanes ont courbé des voiles de bateaux
Et les rames étaient les pattes des chevaux.
Qui veut des calamars, des pieuvres, des rascasses?
Ces poissons ont des dents, des lunettes, des masques
Les toits sont en gradin place du Caïman
Les stores, les balcons le sont également
Peu de fleurs au marché, mais beaucoup de cerises
Les balcons sont embrouillés; comme à Venise
Les stores ont l'air de chemise.
Et des buissons de roses comme la tour de Pise.
La cuisine espagnole sentait un peu le foin

Honor of the Sardana and the Tenora ▬▬▬

Dedicated to Picasso[2]

S EA is the Aegean passing Alicante.[3]
Ah! some have annuities, why can't I?[4]
Mountains keep sea and city safe from harm.
The walls display Castille's coat of arms;[5]
The churches are square, the houses as well.
Thank you's the tale the people's faces tell.
They're Romans from the Opéra-Comique[6]
If ever togas could be comical.
The blue of carneys' blue ties sticking out.
Were prunes the shade of unripe olives, then
Why they'd be prunes, all these severe old men,
These old men are too thin; too fat, these young louts!
The gypsies go to cinematographs
Future goatskin kids have necks just like giraffes
Phrygian Catalans[7] were selling snails
Upon the tartans curled and curved their sails
While their oars were all the hooves of horses.
Who wants squid or octopus or rascasse?[8]
These fish have teeth, they wear glasses or masks
And all the roofs on Caiman Square[9] are terraced
Like the awnings, balconies, and all the rest
Few flowers at market, but lots of cherries
As in Venice the muddled balconies
The awnings look like nighties.
The tower of Pisa's a rosebush like these.
Spanish cuisine does smell a bit like hay

Mais la salle à manger était vraiment mauresque
Si tu n'as jamais vu l'Espagne
Tu ne sais ce que c'est que ville dans campagne.
C'est couleur chocolat ou mieux café au lait
Ou bien c'est blanc dans des montagnes de minerai.
Si tu n'as jamais vu l'Espagne
—Alfred de Musset l'a dit, pour sûr!—
Tu ne sais ce que c'est qu'un mur
Un mur de couvent a des portes cochères
Il en a par devant, il en a par derrière.
Arcades sous les toits, arcades sur la rue.
Dans la journée la ville est nue.
Beaucoup de gens ici sont cireurs de souliers.
Ils jonglent avec la brosse en vous tenant le pied.
Ça n'empêche que sur la citadelle
Deux fois tronquée l'église domine des tourelles.
Il paraît que la forteresse a des canons
Qui garderaient la route du haut de certain mont.
Les soldats sur la tête ont du cuir en canon
Devant dix-huit cafés ils boivent des canons
        La mère et la fille
Ont des éventails. Deux moustaches brillent.
        La mère est en noir
Excepté les cafés en Bourse du Travail
Où beaucoup d'hommes sont en blouse de travail
Les démons du Soleil habitaient tout le reste.
On en avait fermé les volets avec soin.

But then, the dining room was truly Moorish
If you have never been to Spain
Then towns in countryside you can't explain.
They're chocolate colored, or coffee, or
Perhaps they're white among mountains of ore.
If you have never been to Spain
—Alfred de Musset said it all!—[10]
You've never really seen a wall
A convent wall that has a porte-cochère[11]
In front and in back, there's plenty to spare
Arches here beneath the roofs, arches there
Upon the road. By day the city's bare.
A lot of people here polish shoes.
They hold your foot as they juggle the brush.
Even so the twice-truncated
Citadel by church turrets is dominated.
It seems the fortress has canons enough
To guard the road upon a certain bluff.
In leather helmets soldiers bold and bluff
Drink at eighteen cafés, play cards and bluff
     Mother and daughter
Wave fans. Two moustaches show their luster.
     The mother wears black.
Except for cafés as trade union centers,
Where many working men wear overalls
Demons of the Sun reign over all
So they had closed the shutters up with care.

Je me souviendrai toute ma vie de l'instrument de musique qui a nom « Tenora »; c'est long comme une clarinette et ça lutterait, affirme un musicien, avec quarante trombones. Le son en est sec comme celui de la cornemuse. J'ai entendu la « Tenora » à Figueras, ville de la Catalogne, dans un petit orchestre sur la place publique. L'orchestre était composé d'un violoncelle, d'un piston, de cuivres et d'une flûte qui faisait de brefs et charmants soli. On dansait la sardane et avant chaque danse l'orchestre exécutait une longue introduction d'une allure grandiloquente. La déclamation de la « Tenora » était soutenue par les autres instruments bien serrés l'un contre l'autre. Ce sont les musiciens de la ville qui composent cette admirable musique; leurs noms sont inconnus en France excepté de la Maison Pathé frères. Ces fabricants de phonographes ne reculent devant aucun sacrifice quand il s'agit, etc. . . . Après l'introduction, le rythme de la danse commence; ce rythme est d'une solidité telle que je ne crois pas qu'on puisse souhaiter davantage: un rythme de polka coupé de silences brusques, de longues fioritures. Il y a dans la musique des sardanes, des embrasements qui font penser à la splendeur. La sardane se danse en rond, bras en girandoles et presque immobiles, sauf dans les moments d'embrasement. Vous regarderez les pieds des danseurs qui sont tendus et qui exécutent des grimaces gracieuses. Au centre de la ronde, il y a une autre ronde et, au milieu de cette ronde, une autre; et les mouvements de ces rondes sont les mêmes, mais ne coïncident pas, parce que chaque meneur de ronde n'a pas le même sentiment de la musique. Il y avait plusieurs roses de rondes le soir sur le pavé de la place à Figueras.

For the rest of my life I will remember the musical instrument which bears the name "Tenora"; it's long like a clarinet and would hold its own, according to one musician, against forty trombones. It has a dry sound like that of the bagpipes. I heard the "Tenora" in Figueres, a city in Catalonia, in a little band on the public square.[12] The band was composed of a cello, a cornet, brass instruments, and a flute that played brief and charming soli. They would dance the sardana, and before each dance the band would play a long introduction in a grandiloquent manner. The "Tenora's" announcement was supported by the other instruments, packed tightly beside each other. It is the musicians of the city who compose this admirable music; their names are unknown in France with the exception of the Pathé Brothers.[13] These phonograph-makers spare no sacrifice when it comes to, etc. . . . . After the introduction, the rhythm of the dance begins; this rhythm has such solidity that I don't believe any more could be wished for: a polka rhythm punctuated by sudden silences and long flourishes. In the music of the sardana there are flare-ups reminiscent of splendor. The sardana is danced in a circle, arms in wreaths and nearly immobile, except during the flare-ups. You will gaze at the dancers' tensed feet performing graceful grimaces. In the center of the circle, there is another circle and, in the middle of that one, yet another; and the movements of these circles are the same, but do not coincide, because each circle's leader has a different feeling for the music. There were several circling roses on the paving-stones of Figueres' square that evening.

Sardane! tu es comme une rose
Et toutes ces jeunes filles sont en rose.
Il n'y a que les maisons qui ne dansent pas,
Et l'on se demande pourquoi.

La musique a fait pleurer nos yeux
La musique ingénue a gêné nos poitrines,
Comme elle a regonflé le cercle grave et joyeux
Chantez! chantez! chantez! tenoras et clarines.

Le peuple serait comme les vagues de la mer
Si la mer était rose et tournait dans la nuit,
Si la nuit était rose, si rose était la mer
Et si la mer était comme les arbres verts.

Filles des muletiers, gens qui servez à table
Penchez-vous! jetez-vous des regards adorables,
Et par-dessus les bras tendus en candélabres!
Songez à Dieu qui vous regarde dans les arbres

Et par les yeux des boutiques et par la mer.
La tenora fendait la nuit et sa poussière
Nasillarde, comme avec des éclats de verre
La danse roucoulait noblement avec des passements de pied
        allègres.

Chaque instrument se tenait par la taille
Et la tenora dans la musique faisait une entaille.

Sardana! you are like a rose
And the young girls are all dressed in rose.
Only the houses are not dancing
Why not? it leaves us wondering.

The music's brought a tear to the eye
To innocent music the heart swells
Just as the circle's sober mood runs high
Sing! Sing! Sing! the tenoras and the bells.

The people were like the waves of the seas
If the seas were a spinning rose at night
If the night were rose, if rose were the seas
And if the seas themselves were like green trees.

Oh servants' daughters, lowly muleteers
Bow and exchange those loving looks and cheers
Over your arms cast up like chandeliers!
And God, upon you from the trees he peers

And from the eyes of shops, and from the sea.
The tenora split the night's dust, its blast
Nasal, as though with shards of glass
Nobly the dance would trill with gaily braided feet.

Each instrument was cradled by the waist
And through a rent it tore in the music, the tenora raced.

Ainsi que dans une tragédie est un spectre
Qui passe rarement et passe comme un astre
La sèche tenora, trompette nasillarde
Ne bruit que rarement pour de courtes sardanes.

Les fillettes iront se coucher de bonne heure.
Et les hommes seront au café tout à l'heure
Car les musiciens sont payés tant par heure
Quarante pesetas pour donner du bonheur.

Un garçon se plaignait qu'on ne sût plus danser.
Une fille grattait la jambe à son soulier.
Vers la fin, des messieurs et des dames très bien
S'appliquaient du pied gauche et la main dans la main.

Dansez aussi, dame en grand deuil.
Une fille a reçu de la poussière dans l'œil.
Elle va se cacher derrière un réverbère
Où l'attendait sa mère avec les autres mères

Et malgré sa douleur elle sourit encore
Aux accents séduisants de l'ardente ténore.
Les balcons se drapaient des couleurs catalanes
Pendant que tressautait la rose des sardanes.

Le choc du jaune et du rouge s'allie assez
Avec, ô tenora, tes gammes alliacées.
Elle m'a grisé comme une eau-de-vie.

Just as a specter in a tragedy
Will rarely pass, and pass by like a planet
The tenora, this dry and nasal trumpet
Sounds so rarely, for brief sardanas only.

The girls have bedtime at an early hour
The men will find the bar at happy hour
For these musicians' pay is by the hour
Forty pesetas for this happy hour.

A boy complained no one can dance these days.
A girl was scratching her leg near her slipper
Near the end, fine ladies and gentlemen proper
All dance hand in hand as each left foot sways.

Lady in mourning, dance you must.
Into a little girl's eye flies the dust.
She runs away to hide behind a lamp
Her mother's waiting where the mothers camp.

Although she suffers, she will smile for a
Sound so seductive, the ardent tenora.
Houses flew the Catalan colors as
Long as the rose shook, the rose of sardanas.

The yellow and red's colliding ideas
Allied to chromatic allioideaes,[14]
Tenora, how your spirits make me tipsy

Elle s'est éteinte comme une bougie
Son souvenir est dans ma vie.

On dit que l'Empereur a passé par ici
Et qu'on retrouve encor ses soldats dans les puits.
Les soldats ont dansé la sardane en vainqueurs
Couchés derrière ces terrasses, ces géraniums, ces pilastres
Ils ne s'éveillaient plus un poignard dans le cœur.
La sèche tenora a passé comme un astre.

Adieu, sardane et tenora! Adieu, tenoras et sardane
Demain, puisque le sort me damne
Demain puisque le czar l'ordonne
Demain je serai loin d'ici
Demain dans les jardins près de ces monastères
Le peuple sourira pour cacher ses prières
Et moi je te dirai merci!

Snuffed out just like a candle's wispy
Flame, my life contains your memory.

They say the Emperor once passed here[15]
That in the wells his soldiers still appear.
They danced sardanas as they played the part
Of conquerors: asleep behind these porches, geraniums and
    pilasters
They woke no more a dagger through the heart.
Like a planet the dry tenora has departed.

Farewell, tenora and sardana! Farewell, sardana and tenora
Tomorrow, for thus the stars command
Tomorrow for thus the czars condemn
Me to be far from here at daybreak
Tomorrow near this monastery's garden
The people's smile will keep their prayers hidden
And I will give thanks for your sake!

Le départ

ADIEU l'étang et toutes mes colombes
Dans leur tour et qui mirent gentiment
Leur soyeux plumage au col blanc qui bombe
  Adieu l'étang.

Adieu maison et ses toitures bleues
Où tant d'amis, dans toutes les saisons,
Pour nous revoir avaient fait quelques lieues,
  Adieu maison.

Adieu le linge à la haie en piquants
Près du clocher! oh! que de fois le peins-je—
Que tu connais comme t'appartenant
  Adieu le linge!

Adieu lambris! maintes portes vitrées.
Sur le parquet miroir si bien verni
Des barreaux blancs et des couleurs diaprées
  Adieu lambris!

Adieu vergers, les caveaux et les planches
Et sur l'étang notre bateau voilier
Notre servante avec sa coiffe blanche
  Adieu vergers.

Adieu aussi mon fleuve clair ovale,
Adieu montagne! adieu arbres chéris!
C'est vous qui tous êtes ma capitale
  Et non Paris.

The Departure ================

FAREWELL my pond and all my many doves
Upon their tower and who kindly donned
Their silky plumage and its swollen loves
    Farewell pond.

Farewell my home and all its gables blue
So many friends in every season come
To see us, though from leagues away they flew,
    Farewell home.

Farewell laundry! upon a hedge it hangs
I've painted it so often, near the belfry!
—You know it is to you that it belongs
    Farewell laundry!

Farewell wainscot! and many doors of glass.
Upon the mirror floor they shined a lot
With bars of white, whose colors brightly flash
    Farewell wainscot!

Farewell orchards, the cellars and the panels
And on the pond our sailboats just like birds
Our white-coiffed maid along with all the flannels
    Farewell orchards.

Farewell, oval river clearest of all,
Farewell my mountain! Farewell sweet forest!
It's all of you who are my capitol
    And never Paris.

Incertitudes

Hercule enfant trouva deux chemins à sa route
L'un conduisait au vice et l'autre à la vertu.
S'il eût continué l'un, il eût trouvé sans doute
Des bifurcations qui l'eussent confondu.
Faut-il se recueillir loin du monde et chez soi?
Faut-il vivre au dehors afin de plaire aux hommes?
La femme d'un ami qui vous offre la pomme
Se venge si du bien vous observez la loi.
Un écrivain surtout s'embarrasse et se double.
Prend-il un style ici, voilà maints compliments
Prend-il un autre genre? oh! c'est la pluie de roubles
Que faut-il préférer la gloire ou bien l'argent?
Être libre est très beau, mais trop libre en son livre
L'écrivain quelquefois sent le poids de l'azur
Et puis d'avoir glissé sur la ruse du givre
De tout l'hiver peut-être il n'aura le pain sûr.

Uncertainties

Two different routes little Hercules found
One led to vice, the other to virtue.
Had he followed the one, well, it is true
Its twists and turns were enough to confound.
Then must one flee the world and stay at home?
Or live in the world to please humankind?
Your friend's wife gives you an apple to come
And takes revenge if you're not so inclined.
The writer most of all doubts and doubles
For this style, so many compliments
And for another? oh! it rains rubles
Should one prefer glory or endorsements?
To be free is beautiful, but too free
In words the writer feels the azure weight
And fallen on frost's ruse, that winter he
Might not have bread all season on his plate.[16]

Le départ du marin

Dites, algues très douces, adieu vers le bateau
Guère plus gros qu'un ex-voto
De sa fine corde, Neptune à l'horizon
Comme de harpes veut jouer, le gros garçon
Pâmoisons des petites feuilles aristocratiques
Selon ce qu'elles étaient et selon le contraire
Quand il venait avec son air socratique
Causer des ports avec les trois douaniers en vert
Ce bateau si petit pour la mer, le phare l'observe
De son œil de vieillard aveugle et plein de larmes
La sirène des usines de conserves
Jette son cri d'alarme
Le môle qui jadis sentit ses pieds d'enfant
Et le témoin jaloux de chastes fiançailles
Lui qui protégea de rudes embarquements la nuit
Il a voulu parler pour ne pas qu'il s'en aille
Sur le bateau de nacre à l'aurore, fragile
Triste est le cri du paon au château de l'Anglaise
Et tristes les moutons, ces boucles des falaises
Et tout ce qui se croise en l'azur se fait part
Nuage, insecte, oiseau, de son triste départ.
Pas un bruit dans un arbre! lagune! face glabre
La nature se tait! le flot fuit l'horizon.
Sable blanc! Sable blanc! mariage de raison.
Reviens bientôt, dit la fumée
Levant le bras nonchalamment
Reviens! murmure aussi le vent
Et le tumulte du marché

The Seaman's Departure

SAY, sweetest seaweed, farewell toward the boat
Hardly bigger than an ex-voto
With his thin cord, skyward Neptune afloat
As if on harps would play, that big kiddo
Too fond fronds swoon, they're aristocratic
Being as they were, being the reverse
When he showed up with an air so Socratic
To talk of ports with customs officers
So tiny for the sea, the boat this lighthouse surveys
With its weepy old blind man's eye
The siren of the cannery conveys
Its alarm with a cry
The seawall that once felt his childish feet
And the jealous witness at the chaste engagement
He who held back rough boardings in the night
It wished to talk to keep him from leaving
Upon the pearly boat at dawn, so fragile
Sad the peacock's cry at the English Lady's castle
And sad the sheep, those curls upon the cliffs
And all that crosses azure skies is sharing
Cloud, insect, bird, that sadly he is leaving.
Not a sound in a tree! lagoon! glabrous face
Nature speaks not! Waves flee the horizon.
White sand! White sand! an arranged marriage.
Come back soon, says the smoke
Lifting its arm nonchalantly.
Come back! purrs the wind as well
And the market's wild swell

Ne se traduit pas autrement.
      Reviens!
Hurle un certain très pauvre chien
      Reviens!
La servante du Cheval Blanc
Elle porte une bague au doigt
Qu'elle mêle au ruissellement
Des verres et bols qu'elle nettoie
Casimir offrirait sa rose
Las! il sait! il hésite, il n'ose!

Does not translate otherwise.
    Come back!
Yells a certain very wretched dog
    Come back!
The maid at the White Horse
Bears a ring on her hand
Mixed with the water's course
Over bowls and glasses
Casimir would offer his rose
Alas! he doesn't dare! he knows!

Mille regrets

J'AI retrouvé Quimper où sont nés mes quinze premiers ans
Et je n'ai pas retrouvé mes larmes.
Jadis quand j'approchais les pauvres faubourgs blancs
Je pleurais jusqu'à me voiler les arbres.
Cette fois tout est laid, l'arbre est maigre et nain vert
Je viens en étranger parmi des pierres
Mes amis de Paris que j'aime, à qui je dois
D'avoir su faire des livres gâtent les bois
En entraînant ailleurs loin des pins maigres ma pensée
Heureuse et triste aussi d'être entraînée
Plutôt je suis de marbre et rien ne rentre. C'est l'amour
De l'art qui m'a fait moi-même si lourd
Que je ne pleure plus quand je traverse mon pays
Je suis un inconnu: j'ai peur d'être haï
Ces gens nouveaux qui m'ignorent, je crois qu'ils me haïssent
Et je n'ai plus d'amour pour eux: c'est un supplice.

A Thousand Regrets

I came back to Quimper where my first fifteen years were born
And my tears did not come back to me.
When long ago I would come near forlorn
Suburbs, I cried until I couldn't see the trees.
Now it's ugly, the tree is scrawny midget green
Myself a foreigner among the stones that lean
Beloved friends from Paris, those who taught
Me to write, ruin the woods, carrying away,
Far from the scrawny pines my every thought
Both happy and unhappy to be led astray
I am rather made of marble, nothing sticks.
It's love of art has made myself so thick
I cry no longer when I contemplate
My country: I'm a stranger and I fear their hate.
Unknown to these new folk, I fear they hate me
I love them no longer: it torments me.

Plainte du mauvais garçon

JE revois de l'été les persiennes bien closes
 Les persiennes que regrettent les roses
Ah! les grands poissons blancs sur la nappe de verre
La bonne Catherine! et le gars Nicolas!
Le soleil sur l'étang derrière l'usine à gaz
C'est la maladie de l'amour
Qui me retient ici avec des désirs différents
Parmi les démons et les filles de carrefour
      Ah! buvons à la régalade
Encore une de montée dans le panier à salade!

Hooligan's Lament

SHUT Venetian blinds that I remember
And for which the roses pine in summer
Ah! the big white fish on the sheet of glass
Good-hearted Catherine! and Nicky-boy too!
The sun on the pond behind the gas plant
It's the sickness of love
That keeps me here with different desires
Among the demons and the streetwalkers
        Ah! drain a flagon
And that's one more in the paddy wagon!

Nocturne

Entre, déesse, en notre grange
Contemple tes épis vainqueurs
Il ne se peut que tu déranges
Le sommeil des cultivateurs.

Les fleurs parlent bas à la terre
Pour les morts la lune répond
En révélant de sa lumière
Les deux arbres, les quatre maisons.

J'entends chantonner vers les nues
Un rêve qui se fait chanson
Une femme—oh!—toute nue
Dans la grange comme au balcon.

Les serpents endormis faisaient mes initiales
Le concert des animaux se taisaient
Chaque brin d'herbe était un morceau de folie
Et les arbres du fond ignoraient leur beauté.

Nocturne

GODDESS, come inside our garner
And see your ears' triumphant heap
For you cannot cause disorder
To any of these farmers' sleep.

The flowers whisper to the earth
The dead the moon will answer for
Its light, its silver rays unearth
The pair of trees, the houses four.

I hear it sing to altitudes
That dream become a harmony
A lady—oh!—completely nude
In barns as on the balcony.

The sleeping snakes signed with my initials[17]
The animal concert grew quiet
Each blade of grass was a bit of madness
The trees behind knew not of their beauty.

Accès de vue perspective ▬▬▬▬

Vᴜᴇ en montagne d'une maison blanche à tourelles.
C'est la nuit! il y a une fenêtre de lumière,
Il y a deux tourelles, deux tourterelles de tourelles
Derrière la fenêtre et dans la maison
Il y a l'amour, l'amour et sa lumière de feu!
Il y a l'amour à foison, à ailes, à éloquence
Au troisième étage de la maison
Au troisième étage de la maison dans une autre chambre
Chambre sans lumière, il y a un mort
Et toute la douleur de la mort
La moisson de la douleur,
Les ailes de la douleur,
L'éloquence de la douleur
Vue perspective d'une maison blanche à tourelles.

Fit of Perspective View

Mountain outlook on a white house with turrets.
It's nighttime! there's a window of light,
There are two turrets, two turtledove turrets,
Behind the window and in the house
There is love, love and its light of flame!
There is love overflowing, winged, eloquent
On the third story of the house
On the third story of the house in another room
A room without light, there is a dead man
And all the suffering of death
The harvest of suffering,
The wings of suffering,
The eloquence of suffering
Perspective view of a white house with turrets.

Les volontaires espagnols quittent Paris ▬▬▬▬

LES sciences ont eu longtemps l'empire de la terre.
Leur empire n'est plus; voici venir la guerre.
Le président de France était le plus savant
Et jadis il avait instruit les jeunes gens
Les honneurs qu'on rendait aux savants étaient tels
Qu'on les faisait mourir pour les rendre immortels
Ils prenaient du thé russe en des salons charmants
Et décernaient des prix aux plus intelligents
Ils accueillaient les gars instruits de tous les mondes
Quand ils avaient prouvé leur féconde faconde.
Paris était alors le gros centre du monde.
On venait à Paris de tous les points du monde
Les inventeurs étaient promptement enrichis
Il en était de bons et bien d'autres aussi
Les médecins étaient honorés comme dieux:
Il y en avait pour la gorge et les yeux
Il y en avait pour la bouche et les oreilles
Pour les dents, les cheveux, les genoux, les orteils
Il y en avait pour le ventre et l'estomac
Le tube digestif et ce qui est plus bas
On en avait pour le cœur et pour le foie
Et sur d'autres autels on riait de la foi
Le seul théologien était François de Sales
Le plus accommodant en matière de morale
Quand les savants avaient prononcé leurs oracles
Les pharmaciens faisaient à loisir des miracles
C'était toujours avec politesse et douceur
On était ironique, on n'avait pas de cœur

The Spanish Volunteers Leave Paris

Though science long has reigned over the land,
It reigns no longer, for war is at hand.
The French president was learned in truth
And long ago he instructed the youth
The honors for those learned men would startle
You: they let them die to make them immortal
They took Russian tea in quite charming parlors
Bestowed their prizes on the smartest scholars
They welcomed well-read guys from every city
Once proved their prolific prolixity.
Paris was then the center of the world
People came from everywhere in the world
Inventors were promptly made rich and so
There were the good ones and others also
Doctors were honored like gods: there were some
Just for the eyes and the throat, and then come
Some more for the mouth, the ears, and the nose,
For the teeth and hair as well as the toes
There were some for the stomach and torso
The digestive tract, for what lies below
More for the heart and still more for the liver
For all other faiths they laughed on the altar
The sole theologian was François de Sales[18]
In moral matters most human in scale
The learned would publish their oracles
As pharmacists performed their miracles
And always politely, with gentleness
Yet ironic in spirit, and heartless

Et cætera, et cætera, et cætera.
Mais les temps vont changer; nous n'en sommes plus là.
Voici que les ballons se croisent dans la nue
Voici que les soldats se croisent dans la rue
Brûlez vos parchemins nous en savons assez
Pour panser la blessure et pour fondre l'acier.
Acheter! vendre! jouir! non! non! coupons les têtes
Le beau sang va couler aux cris de la trompette
Les nations avaient besoin de plus d'espace.
De mille esprits brillants il faut faire une glace
Le temps n'est plus des grades, des fortunes, des places
Revenez de Paris pour fortifier nos places.
Allons! jeunes savants, formez vos bataillons!
Et recouvrez vos malles avec nos pavillons.
Que nos drapeaux flottants illuminent les gares
Elle est brodée de fleurs, d'animaux, votre épée
Soldats de notre chère Méditerranée
Va! pars tirer de l'arc en nos guerres puniques
« Renoncer à ma chaire de mathématiques!
Quand la sève des foules aux reflets incertains
Montait à rebrousse poil des leçons de latin
Je ne te soupçonnais pas encore
Ivresse en troisième classe des drapeaux tricolores
Tu m'as fait oublier, Paris, jusqu'à mon nom!
Mes taureaux, mes danses, mon titre d'hidalgo
Le cœur de nos instituteurs
N'est pas celui de nos sultanes.
Il est moins beau et moins trompeur.

Et cetera, et cetera, et cetera.
But times change; it's a different era.
For now the balloons cross paths in the clouds
And the soldiers cross paths in the roads
Burn your parchments, we know enough to heal
A wound, we know enough to melt down steel.
Buy! sell! party! no! let's cut off a head
At the trumpet's cry the streets will run red
The nations needed a good deal more space.
Of a thousand brilliant minds let's make ice[19]
It's not time for rank, fortune, pride of place,
From Paris, come and fortify the place.
Let's go, young learned men, form your battalions!
And cover your baggage with our pavilions.
May our flags fly and light up the stations
Beasts, blossoms embroider your guardian
Swords, soldiers of our Mediterranean
Go! leave and be an archer in this Punic
War: "Give up my chair in mathematics!
When the sap of crowds that glints uncertain
Rose up against my lessons in Latin
I didn't suspect you yet
Boozing of third class in tricolor flags
Paris, my name you have made me forget
My bulls, my dances, my title—hidalgo
The hearts of our schoolteachers
Are not that of our sultanas.
They have less lovely, less deceitful features.

C'est le métro pour la tartane! »
Débris d'un univers, poussière des bouquins,
Nous sommes dans les prés entraînés par les trains.
Charbons ardents sous l'œil indulgent de la foule
Les pillards déjà suivaient l'armée scolaire.
Ainsi que devant l'eau qui monte l'on recule
On avait tout vendu pour partir à la guerre:
Ateliers de génie, microscopes et livres.
Aux portes des wagons on en vendait encore
Et même on en donnait car plusieurs étaient ivres
Et l'on changeait aussi des armes contre l'or

Écho d'écho si tu m'entraînes
Dolent sous le bleu firmament
C'est au service de ma reine
Fais-moi voir aussi ma maman

Le courlis ne se prend qu'en plaine
Je l'ai bien chassé dans le temps!
     —L'étang—
Ainsi le veut ma souveraine
Nous saurons chasser le Birman

À tous buffets, de toutes gares
Nous irons chanter des péans
Demain, mourons! aujourd'hui gare!
Ne tachons pas nos pantalons

It's the metro in place of tartanas!"[20]
A world's debris, books and their dust remain
And into the fields we're taken by train.
Hot coals beneath the crowd's indulgent gaze
The looters crept behind the bookish force.
Before the waters rising one gives way
And so had all been sold to go to war:
Engineers' workshops, microscopes and books.
In front of wagons they were being sold
A few being drunk, thefts were overlooked
For weapons too they gave away their gold

Echo echoing if I am seen
Marching doleful beneath the blue weather
It is in the service of my queen
But I also wish to see my mother

The curlew is caught in the plains alone
I hunted it so well in yesteryear!
        —the mere—
These are the wishes of my sovereign
For whom we'll hunt the Burman far and near

At all buffets and from every station
We'll march and sing a hymn
Tomorrow we'll die, today, attention!
But keep your trousers trim

Pierpont Morgan, le milliardaire
Donne des fonds pour les blessés
Ma nourrice est infirmière
Elle en touchera la moitié.

Avril 1910

Pierpont Morgan, the billionaire[21]
Gives money for the injured men
My nanny offers nurse's care
And she'll take half the cash he sends.

April 1910

À M. Modigliani pour lui prouver que je suis un poète

Le nuage est la poste entre les continents
Syllabaire d'exil et que les Océans,
Condamnés par l'Enfer à se battre en pleurant
N'épèleront pas sur le vernis de l'espace.
Le noir sommet des monts s'endort sur les terrasses
Sillons creusés par Dieu pour cacher les humains
Sans lire le secret du nuage qui passe
Lui ne sait pas non plus ce que portent ses mains
Mais parfois lorsque son ennemi le vent le chasse
Il se tourne, rugit et lance un pied d'airain.
J'étais, enfant, doué. Mille reflets du ciel
Promenaient, éveillé, les charmes de mes songes,
Et venaient éclipser l'étendard du réel.
Au milieu mes amis, enseignés par les anges
J'ignorais qui j'étais et j'écrivais un peu.
Au lieu de femme un jour j'avais rencontré Dieu
Compagnon qui brode mon être
Sans que je puisse le connaître.
Il est le calme et la gaîté
Il donne la sécurité
Et pour célébrer ses mystères
Il m'a nommé son secrétaire
Or pendant les nuits je déchiffre
Un papier qu'il chargea de chiffres
Que de sa main même il écrit
Et déposa dans mon esprit
Dans l'aquarium des airs vivent les démons indiscrets
Qui font écrouler le nuage pour lui voler notre secret.

To M. Modigliani to Prove to Him I Am a Poet ▬▬

A cloud is intercontinental mail
Syllabary of exile that Seas fail,
Seas Hell condemned to beat themselves and wail,
Fail to spell upon the polish of space.
The black peaks fall asleep upon the place
Where God cut furrows to hide mankind
Unable to read the cloud's passing face
It knows no better what its hand may find
Yet sometimes when the wind would chase
It, it will cast its iron heel behind.
As a child I was gifted and the sky
Would then parade my charming reverie
Eclipsing pennants of reality.
In the middle my friends to angels nigh,
I knew not who I was, and wrote a bit.
Instead of a wife it was God I met
This unknowable company
Who stitches my embroidery.
He is calm, he is gaiety
And he provides security
To celebrate his mystery
He's named me his secretary
Now, in the night I decipher
His page with many a cipher
Of his sole hand itself the writ
Deposited in my spirit
In the air's aquarium live nosy demons
Who cave in the cloud to steal our secret within.

Passé et present ━━━━━━━━

Poète et ténor
L'oriflamme au nord
Je chante la mort.

Poète et tambour
Natif de Colliour
Je chante l'amour.

Poète et marin
Versez-moi du vin
Versez! versez! Je divulgue
Le secret des algues.

Poète et chrétien
Le Christ est mon bien
Je ne dis plus rien.

Past and Present

P OET and tenor
Banner to the fore
I sing of death's door.

Poet kettle drum
Native to Epsom[22]
I sing love's ransom.

Poet and seafarer
Pour me some liquor
Pour me some more! I relate
The seaweed's secret.

Poet repentant
Christ my availment
Now I am silent.

Le citadin mort à l'amour de la nature lui adresse ses adieux

DE longues voix d'enfants percent le crépuscule.
Avec le télégraphe elles semblent courir
Les regrets opulents du soleil qui recule
Dorent le sable pâle où le flot vient mourir
Je meurs de ton glacial exil, ô Déesse!
Essaim d'échos la flûte invite à la tristesse
Je meurs de te connaître et meurs de t'ignorer
Je te donne ma chair et c'est pour t'adorer
Feuillage, oiseaux attachés qui feuillolent
Feuille qui tombe quand l'un essaie son vol
Forêts, vastes herbiers d'un divin herboriste
Je vous donne mon cœur pour être en ex-libris
Fleur, effort sans regret pour atteindre l'esprit
L'aubier a ton secret, ô lune, astre sans vie
Chaque racine d'arbre est le centre du monde
La mort de chaque plante empoisonne un démon.
Je meurs de ton glacial exil ô déesse.
Essaim d'échos, la flûte invite à la tristesse
Calixte, mon berger, n'appelez pas les Muses
Je veux mourir sans les avoir connues.
Qu'on baisse le rideau de lierre, cette grotte
Doit être le tombeau que la douleur m'apporte.
Abandonnez au sol cette urne, humble trophée
Qu'un agreste concours valut à l'art d'Orphée
Un nouveau site éclate aux bornes du sépulcre:
Les tristes encorbellements de la nature.
Comme un languide amour sur les dalles d'onyx
J'irai porter des fleurs aux sombres eaux du Styx

The City-Dweller Who Died for Love of Nature Gives It His Farewell

L ONG children's voices pierce right through dusk's shade.
And with the telegraph they seem to run
The rich regrets of the retreating sun
Gild the pale sand where ocean waters fade
I die of your glacial exile, o Goddess!
The flute, a swarm of echoes, brings me sadness
I die to know you, or heedless of you
And my flesh I offer to adore you
Foliage, fettered birds covered in leaves[23]
A leaf that falls when one attempts to leave
Woods, albums of a godly botanist
I give my heart to be your ex-libris
A flower, reaching no regrets for spirit
Sapwood knows your secret, dead lunar planet
Every tree root is the world's true center
Each plant's death is a demon's poisoner.
I die of your glacial exile o Goddess.
The flute, a swarm of echoes, brings me sadness
Calixte,[24] my shepherd, do not call the Muses
I want to die without having known them.
Let down the ivy curtain, for this grotto
Must be the tomb that suffering brings me to.
Leave to the ground this urn, humble trophy, as
The country contest granted Orpheus
A new site rises up before the sepulcher:
The melancholy corbel vaults of nature.
Like a languid lover on the slabs of onyx
I shall bring flowers to the waters of the Styx

Mais toi, roi de l'Oubli, ô fleuve du Léthé
Je te jette en défi les splendeurs de l'été,
Comme s'étale encore au pied d'une colonne
Le voile de l'inspiration qui t'abandonne
J'emporte dans la tombe un lambeau de l'azur.
Le ruisseau des vergers dans le vallon obscur
Le houx dont les épis escaladent le ciel
Le couchant qui fait les monts bleus couleur de miel
Or, pour dresser au chêne un support de cristal
Les rocs ont découpé leur front monumental.
Ô nature étrangère et qui nous vient d'ailleurs!
J'ignore sa patrie, elle ignore mon cœur
D'où viens-tu, l'herbe? Qui donc es-tu, l'espace?
Je meurs en étranger, ô terre à jamais lasse!
Cybèle, je t'aimais sans t'avoir reconnue
Et je vais pour toujours mourir sur ton sein nu
Où tu me retiendras sans vouloir me connaître.
Meurs! va résoudre au Styx les énigmes de l'Être
Meurs! Daphné, du secret d'Apollon confidente.
Tremble aussitôt qu'on dort de l'approche des plantes.

But you, Oblivion's king, Lethe, o river
I throw down the challenge of the summer
Splendors, still spreading at the foot of columns
The veil of inspiration as it's leaving you
I carry to the tomb a shred of heaven's blue.
The orchard's brook down in a darkened vale
The shoots of holly, bit by bit they scale
The sky, where sunsets make the blue peaks pale
As honey; and to prop up oaks in crystal, how
The rocks have cut their monumental brow.
O foreign nature, from some other place!
I do not know its country, nor it my heart.
From where do you come, grass? What are you, space?
I die a stranger, never weary earth!
I loved you, Cybele, but did not see you there,
And I shall die forever more against your bare
Breast, where you will hold me, though not your own.
Die! Go and solve the riddles of being, alone
At the Styx, die! Daphne, Apollo's confidante.[25]
Now tremble in your sleep at the approach of plants.

Pronostics

UNE couverture de laine au bas d'un tuyau vert
Le mât pousse, il grandit, c'est un arbre vert
il monte sous un ciel de nuages gris;
il a une blessure de moisissure sombre au côté.
Sous la couverture de laine, comme une vieille sous un
        capuchon
il y a un squelette dont on ne voit que le crâne,
un crâne dont on ne voit que le front
un front incliné vers sa large pensée
et cette pensée inclinée vers le papier et la plume du squelette
sous la couverture en triangle
le mât pousse vers le ciel gris, il s'épanouit
c'est le bouquet d'un palmier—ah! ah! évoheh
les feuilles touffues d'un palmier, à doigts, à pattes, à mains.
Ces mille éventails d'un palmier sur la fumée du ciel gris
d'un palmier transplanté de l'Afrique du Nord à Paris.

Prognostics

A wool blanket at the foot of a green pipe
The mast grows, lengthens, it's a green tree
it rises beneath a cloudy sky of gray;
a dark lesion of mold marks its flank.
Under the wool blanket, like an old woman in a hood
there are bones whose skull alone is visible
a skull whose brow alone is visible
a brow slanted toward vast considerations
and those considerations slanted toward the bones' pen and
    paper
under the triangular blanket
the mast grows toward the gray sky, it blossoms
it's a palm-tree bouquet—ah! ah! evoheh![26]
the bushy leaves of a palm tree, fingers, paws, hands.
These thousand palm-tree fans against a gray sky's smoke
of a palm tree transplanted from North Africa to Paris.

Ô mes écrits nouveaux! je veux qu'ils outrepassent
Le ciel! le poète fidèle à son rêve impossible!
Attelé dans les bras solides de la Muse
Il écrit sur l'azur envers du Paradis.
Gentil Quimper, le nid de mon enfance
De lierre, ormeaux, roches tout tapissé,
Vois ce, d'un tendre effort, qu'à ta face
J'offre! un miroir de hêtres et de houx,
Hêtres et houx cachant nos jeux de courses
Par intervalle dans l'étroite vallée!
Ayant confié le cartable à la mousse
Avec les compagnons j'ai folâtré.
Mère ou servante, le dos à la feuillée
Brodait, cousait ou ravaudait les bas
Sans craindre trop la pente ravinée
Car les quinconces protégeaient nos faux pas.
Du haut en bas ce n'était que feuillage
Piécettes d'ombre et pièces de soleil
Sur une haie c'est du linge qui flotte
Troupeau gardé par la vieille au bâton
Nous, lévriers de la terre moussue
Nous poursuivions dans les couloirs de hêtres
Blancs, hérissés parfois d'éventails de rameaux
En bas, l'Odet aux ponts de fer multiples
Se gargarise interminablement.
Sur le disque éclatant de l'Odet élargi
J'aimais apercevoir entre les doigts des arbres
Les joues du grand voilier dorées par le soleil

Quimper

O my new writings! Would that they surpass
The sky! The poet true to his impossible dream!
He's harnessed in the Muse's mighty arms
Writes on the azure back of Paradise.
Sweet Quimper, nest of my childhood
All carpeted in ivy, elm, and rock,
Behold, before your face this tender effort
Offered! beeches and holly as a mirror,
The beech and holly hide our games of tag
At intervals within the narrow valley!
My satchel then entrusted to the moss,
With my companions I would frolic.
Her back to the green, a mother or maid
Embroidering or sewing, darning socks
And mostly unafraid of furrowed slopes
For the quincunxes[27] kept us from missteps.
There was only foliage high and low
Spots of shade and bands of sun
Upon a hedge some laundry floats
The crone and her crook keep a flock
And as for us, hounds of the mossy earth
We pursued[28] in the beech tree halls
So white, bristling at times with leafy fans
Below, the Odet's[29] many iron bridges
Gargles on interminably.
The bright disk where the Odet widens out
Is where I liked to see between the fingers
Of trees the cheeks of great sun-golden sailboats

Tandis que sous nos pieds s'élançant des broussailles
Les trois-mâts fins et lourds faisaient songer à Dieu.
J'écris nos deux clochers en lettres majuscules
Fleuries, enrubannées, pleines de cris d'oiseaux
L'escalier de la tour au milieu des coquilles
Des blancs, des nuits, des coins et des coups d'air soudains
C'était comme paraphe! Avec des Parisiens
Nous avons effrayé vos poutres, grandes orgues!
Jésus habite en bas. C'est une tiare
Le haut, le phare que les archanges
Tiennent depuis des siècles et des siècles à deux mains
On tolère la canne et le pied des humains
Or le vallon serait un clocher à l'envers
Sans les gros marronniers et vingt-cinq ponts de fer.

As bursting from the brush beneath our feet
The triple-masted ships brought God to mind.
I write in capitals our double belfries
Flowered, ribboned, full of the cries of birds
The tower stairwell all amidst the shells
Blanks, nights, corners, and sudden bursts of air
As a signature it was! With Parisians
We've startled your beams, grand organs!
Jesus lives below. It's a tiara
Up high, the beacon that archangels
Have held for centuries and more, two-handed
Human feet and canes are tolerated there
The vale might be a belfry in reverse
Were it not for chestnut trees and bridges.

À propos des mépris et des méprises de M. X . . . ▬

Qu'un autre écrive ton histoire, ô Zénobie!
   Dessiner au pastel des pantins sur la moire
Avec de gros marrons grillés jouer aux billes:
Voilà l'occupation de toutes mes soirées.
Non! jamais couronné de jetons de présence
Donnant à mon peplum grâce et désinvolture
Je ne mettrai la muse en bouillon de culture,
Pour avoir trop goûté, messieurs, vos préséances!
Au chêne lauré d'or préférons la fougère
Laquelle est d'une indépendance exagérée
Creusons le sol pour trouver le grand électrique
Et du vulgum pecus méprisons la critique.

Concerning Derisions and Misprisions of Monsieur X . . .

L ET them tell your tale, oh Zenobia!³⁰
Drawing puppets on satin in pastels
With grilled chestnuts playing marbles, this be a:
Pastime made to fill my every evening.
No! never, crowned with tokens of presence
Giving my peplum grace and sprezzatura,
I shall not breed the muse in live culture,
Knowing, Sirs, your system of precedence!
To the laureled oak, we'll prefer the fern
Which is of excessive independence
Let us dig for the grand electrical
And spurn the masses when they're critical.

Mort morale

L<small>A</small> révolution inquiète la patrie
Et des gouttes de feu pleuvent sur les balcons:
Modes, chemiserie, marchands de quat'saisons
Teints du sang des cochers ferment leurs batteries
On n'arrosera plus; les pavés sont tout blancs
Et les chiens fouillent les ordures du printemps
Aux restes dévastés qui furent le Pont-Neuf
Un drapeau sourd et muet dont les plis sont tout neufs
En silence a conduit tes disciples, Babeuf
Dans le Louvre les tableaux incendiés se pourlèchent.
La Tour Eiffel dans l'eau désaltère sa flèche.
La Chambre est occupée militairement,
Une automobile grise emporte des dolmans.
Notre-Dame paraît au creux d'un incendie
Transparente et coulant comme un sucre candi.
Au mont-de-piété les Rothschild font la queue,
L'empereur en uniforme est traîné par les cheveux.
Les matelas crevés sont la langue des murs.
Les pavés impuissants à panser les blessures
Ont le cœur plus humain que les graves passants.
Des supplices chinois place de la Concorde,
Des bourgeois sont pendus à leur porte-manteaux,
On les descend dans la vidange avec des cordes.
Les moines du Carmel sauvant l'Hostie Divine
Dans la rue Quincampoix rencontrent la marine.
Un pensionnat muré est devenu harem,
Les mères des enfants pleuraient devant la porte.
On les a fait saoûler dans un mortel dilemme

Moral Death[31]

REVOLUTION worries our nation
On balconies the flaming droplets fall:
Street vendors and shirt boutiques and fashion
Stained with the blood of coachmen close each stall
Watering is over, the white stone grime-
Free, dogs rummage through the trash of springtime.
To the ruins that once were the Pont-Neuf[32]
A deaf-mute flag whose folds are new enough
In silence led your disciples, Babeuf[33]
The Louvre: burning pictures lick the art
In water Eiffel's tower dips its dart
The Chamber's full of military men,
While a gray car bears away some dolmans.[34]
Notre-Dame juts from the flames that are burning,
Transparent, dripping, like rock candy melting.
At the pawnshop the Rothschilds stand in line,
In uniform the emperor looks fine
Dragged by the hair. Split-open beds against
The walls are tongues. Unfit to ease the torments
Of the wounded, paving stones seem more human
Than the grave passersby. There's Chinese torture
For the bourgeois at place de la Concorde,
They're hanged from their coat racks, dropped with a cord
Into sewage. Saving the holy Host,
Carmelites rue Quincampoix[35] meet a host
Of sailors, and the boarding school's become a
Harem; children's mothers weep at the gate.
Forced to drink, in a mortal dilemma,

On a fait boire les fils près de leurs mères mortes.
Pourquoi tout dire? un jour le Christ est venu
Dans la nue sur la ville, il était nu.
Des anges soutenaient sa couronne, le ciel était fendu.

Sons grew drunk near the bodies of their late
Mothers. Why say it all? One day the air
Brought Christ upon a cloud, his body bare
The heavens split, and angels followed for his crown to bear.

Établissement d'une communauté au Brésil ▬▬

On fut reçu par la fougère et l'ananas
L'antilope craintif sous l'ipécacuanha.
Le moine enlumineur quitta son aquarelle
Et le vaisseau n'avait pas replié son aile
Que cent abris légers fleurissaient la forêt.
Les nonnes labouraient. L'une d'elles pleurait
Trouvant dans une lettre un sujet de chagrin
Un moine intempérant s'enivrait de raisin.
Et l'on priait pour le pardon de ce péché
On cueillait des poisons à la cime des branches
Et les moines vanniers tressaient des urnes blanches.
Un forçat évadé qui vivait de la chasse
Fut guéri de ses plaies et touché de la grâce:
Devenu saint, de tous les autres adoré,
Il obligeait les fauves à leur lécher les pieds.
Et les oiseaux du ciel, les bêtes de la terre
Leur apportaient à tous les objets nécessaires.
Un jour on eut un orgue au creux de murs crépis
Des troupeaux de moutons qui mordaient les épis
Un moine est bourrelier, l'autre est distillateur
Le dimanche après vêpre on herborise en chœur.

Saluez le manguier et bénissez la mangue
La flûte du crapaud vous parle dans sa langue
Les autels sont parés de fleurs vraiment étranges
Leurs parfums attiraient le sourire des anges,
Des sylphes, des esprits blottis dans la forêt
Autour des murs carrés de la communauté.

Establishment of a Community in Brazil

THE fern and the pineapple showed us right in; a
   Skittish antelope beneath ipecacuanha.
The illuminating monk left his colored ink
And the vessel had not yet folded up its wing
When a hundred feather homes blossomed in the woods
The nuns labored. One of them would
Weep, finding in a letter some cause for chagrin
An intemperate monk got drunk on grapes.
And there were prayers to forgive that sin
Poisons were gathered at the tops of branches
And some other monks wove white wicker urns.
Having escaped and surviving on game a slave
Was healed of his wounds, and touched by grace, he was saved:
He became a saint adored by all others there,
He made the wild beasts come to lick their feet,
And the birds of the heavens, the earth's living things
Would bring to each of them any necessity.
One day they heard an organ in the stucco walls
Of flocks of sheep that gnawed on all
The ears. One monk's a saddler, one distills liquors
Their choir gathers plants after Sunday vespers.

Salute the mango tree and bless the mango
The flute of the toad, it can speak your lingo
Flowers truly strange grace the altars while
Their scent would attract the angels' smile,
That of sylphs and spirits tucked in the woods
Around the settlement's right-angled walls

Or voici qu'un matin quand l'Aurore saignante
Fit la nuée plus pure et plus fraîche la plante
La forêt où la vigne au cèdre s'unissait,
Parut avoir la teigne. Un nègre paraissait
Puis deux, puis cent, puis mille et l'herbe en était teinte
Et le Saint qui pouvait dompter les animaux
Ne put rien sur ces gens qui furent ses bourreaux.
La tête du couvent roula dans l'herbe verte
Et des moines détruits la place fut déserte
Sans que rien dans l'azur ne frémît de la mort.

C'est ainsi que vêtu d'innocence et d'amour
J'avançais en traçant mon travail chaque jour
Priant Dieu et croyant à la beauté des choses
Mais le rire cruel, les soucis qu'on m'impose
L'argent et l'opinion, la bêtise d'autrui
Ont fait de moi le dur bourgeois qui signe ici.

Now, here is morning when the bleeding dawn
Made the mists purer and the plant-life cooler;
The forest where were wed the vine and cedar
Seemed to have ringworm. A negro appeared
Then two, a hundred, thousands; coloring the grass
And the Saint who knew how to tame the beasts
Against his killers nothing could be done.
The head of the cloister rolled in green grass
And of monks destroyed the place was deserted
While nothing trembled in the azure heavens.

Thus, clothed in love and innocence I went
Tracing my labors every day: I spent
Them praying to God, believing in beauty
But cruel laughter and all of my worry
Money, judgment, the foolishness of many
Have made the hard bourgeois who signs these lines.

Cancale, le crépuscule

à Claude Benoiste

L E ciel a pour la mer des regards qui bénissent
Le soleil sur la mer est un bateau qui glisse
Chaque lame a son or, chaque écume a sa nuit
Le flot donne un mot d'ordre à la vague qui suit
Le soleil abandonne un soleil qui se brise
Sur le sable, aux endroits où la mer se dérobe
Retenant d'un seul flot cent cercles irisés
Tout plat comme un miroir et vert comme une robe.
Le peuplier divin et robuste, le tremble
Léger, dentelé par l'automne, le pin semblent,
Blessés par le couchant, pour s'endormir ensemble,
Attendre le retour des navires en feu
Or, parmi l'éventail des rochers, c'est un jeu
Des voiles empourprées et des yoles de marbre
D'apparaître après une éclipse encor plus claires.

Mon Claude, nous voici dans la falaise et sous les arbres.
Le télescope de ton vénérable père
S'obstine à rechercher le littoral d'Avranches.
Sur un appareil et sur ses deux mains blanches
Madame la comtesse abaisse la paupière.
Tu demandes qu'un jour mon fragile pinceau
Fasse vivre pour nous un souvenir si beau
Et ma lyre aujourd'hui te répond et l'éveille.

Cancale, Twilight[36] ▬▬▬▬▬

For Claude Benoiste[37]

To bless the sea the sky's gaze takes a dip
  Upon the sea the sun's a gliding ship
Each breaker has its gold, all foam its night
The swell commands the next wave to alight
The sun, it leaves behind a sun that shatters
On the sand, wherever the sea dies down
Holding back a hundred prismed circles
Flat as a mirror and green as a gown.
The poplar divine and robust, the aspen
Light and autumn-laced, the pine, they seem in
Sync, wounded by the sunset; near to sleeping
As they await returning ships in flame
Among the fanned-out rocks it is a game
For scarlet-blushing sails and marble skiffs
When they reappear to seem still more clear.

Dear Claude, here we are beneath the trees on cliffs.
Your venerable father's telescope
Stubbornly seeks the coast, Avranches' sands.[38]
On this device and on her two white hands
Madame the countess closes both her eyes.
You ask my fragile paintbrush that it may
One day for us this memory inspirit:
Today my lyre answers you and wakes it.

L'Explorateur

Aн! tout est arrangé!
Renonce à l'automnal des buissons orangés
Misère de misère! oui tout est arrangé
Tu peux filer ton nœud et courir ta marée.
Ah! ah! éheu! hélas! comme aurait dit Homère
Tu n'as pas un ami, tu n'as père ni mère!
Je suis le brancardier d'un hôpital de fous
Un aveugle blêmi dont la moëlle a des poux
Le Vasco de Gama des plus sombres études.
Je suis embastillé trente ans comme Latude
Ah! fleurissez là-bas, mes beaux marronniers
Votre plus cher amant par vous est renié.

Côtes, coteries, échos des côtes et des cottages
Des cottages et des boycottages!
La belle-mère amère du maire!
Ne point déplaire à ces bergères
Ou crains des représailles sévères.
Tout ce qu'abandonna de sa bande Amanda.
Héphestion maupiteux régalant sa pituite
Percinet préférant au trois-six le trois-huit
Monsieur de Montserrat élu récipiendaire
Et qui braillant sans verve force un autre à se taire
Poupon, roi des grenus, interprète de songes
Et Gaster le Breton triste comme un oronge
Madame Ixe qui cherche un improbable amant
Sachant l'espéranto, Coleridge, Sheridan
Ah! tout est arrangé, vous! fleurissez là-bas mes beaux
    marronniers.

The Explorer

A<small>H</small>! Everything's arranged!
Give up autumnal bushes orange-red
Misery of misery! All is set aside
You can slip your knot and run with your tide.
Oh! o, eheu! alas! says Homer
You have no friends, no father nor mother!
For this asylum I'm the stretcher-bearer
A pallid blind man whose marrow has lice
The Vasco de Gama of darkest arts
Some thirty years secluded like Latude[39]
Ah! flower there, my lovely chestnut boughs
Your lover most dear your heart disavows.

Coasts, coteries, echoes of coasts and cottages
Cottages and cots and boycottages!
Mayor's embittered mom-in-law!
Do not irk the shepherdesses
Or suffer the consequences!
All those abandoned from Amanda's band.
Piteous Hephaestion's[40] pituitary treats
Percinet[41] prefers to eight-balls eight-hour beats
Monsieur de Montserrat[42] received the Fellowship
And ranting coarsely forces someone to shut up
Poupon, dream-interpreter, king of granita[43]
Gaster the Breton like a sad Amanita[44]
Madame Aix seeking some improbable darling
Fluent in Esperanto, Coleridge, The Darling[45]
Ah! Everything's arranged! you! Flower there, my lovely
        chestnut boughs.

Terre arrosée

Dans les verts brouillards de l'Aurore
Ah! tout ce qui se cache, ce qui se cache de bonheur
Et de malheur. Dans les brouillards de la nuit
Le rose ne s'est pas évanoui
Que le chien déjà bâille et s'ennuie.
Il y a autant d'oiseaux que de feuilles dans la forêt.

La nuit quand je pense à la poésie
Je ne peux pas, je ne peux pas dormir
Eau d'aurore
Les mots, ne les dissipez pas encore
—Tu les trouveras dans la rue
En allant revoir tes amis:
Entre le grand ciel triste et tout ce qui, gonflé,
Soupire, le miracle naîtra de la terre arrosée.

Earth After the Rain

IN the green fog of Aurora
Ah! all of what's hidden, what's hidden of happiness
And unhappiness. In the fog of the night
The pink is not yet out of sight
And already the dog yawns and grows bored.
There are as many birds as leaves in the forest.

At night when I think of poetry
I cannot, I cannot sleep
Dawn waters
Do not wash the words away, not yet
—You will find them in the street
As you go to see your friends:
Between the great, sad sky and all the wet
that sighs, from rain the earth will bear the miracle.

Symbolique égyptienne

Un oiseau couleur de noix
  Avec un bec d'oiseau de proie
Passe un gué de sable blanc
Il le tient entre ses ventres
L'eau dévale d'un côté
L'eau dévale un autre pan
Il fera tant et tant
Qu'il passera le versant
Son bec est tout noir dedans.

Egyptian Symbolism

A bird the color of teak
With a bird of prey's curved beak
Passes a ford of white sand
Holding it amidst its midst
Water pitches to one side
Water pitches further and
Further still the bird will slide
It will pass the great divide
Its beak is black inside.

Tapisserie très ancienne ▬▬▬▬▬▬

Deux chevaliers se disputent la dame
Leurs deux chevaux en sont épouvantés.
Dans le soleil on voit briller les lames
Sur les buissons luire les boucliers.

La dame a fui près de certain ermite
Son chien par son voile blanc la retient
Le saint vieillard lui prédit une suite
D'amours sanglants aux lignes de sa main.

Or dans le ciel paraît un hippogriffe,
C'est son fiancé gentilhomme et breton
Qui de la lune aux ordres d'un calife
Revient avec l'herbe de la Raison.

Un vieux seigneur habite les tourelles
D'un haut château paré d'un mur d'acier
La cour d'amour y joue du violoncelle
Le vieux seigneur est très hospitalier.

Saints Pierre et Jean, tout ce monde surveille
Les Anges vont viennent en estafiers.
Dans les enfers du siège de Marseille
Se soucient le Diable et ses conseillers.

Very Ancient Tapestry

Two knights' dispute concerns a maid
And thus their pair of horses scare
Beneath the sun they shine, the blades
The shields upon the shrubs, they glare.

The lady's fled to find a hermit
As by her veil her dog holds on
To the old saint her hands admit
The bloody loves she'll fall upon.

Then overhead a hippogriff
Flies, it is her love, a Breton
Sent to the moon by a caliph
Carrying the herb of Reason.

There lived a lordly old fellow
Behind a castle's walls of steel
There the court of love plays cello
He welcomes everyone with zeal.

All these Saint Pierre and John survey
Angels come, go as men-at-arms.
In hell on the seat of Marseilles
The Fiend and friends sound their alarms.

L'Aurore

Qui attend le Seigneur au matin de nacre?
L'herbe humide et noire, l'arbre et son mystère
On a préparé tous les bocages pour le Sacre.
Les feuilles engourdies que la froide nuit gerce.

L'Amour soulève les rideaux de la nuit,
L'Amour épand des roses au chevet du lit
On a pillé la roseraie.

La mer est blonde, ronde comme un ciel,
Le ciel est rond comme une baie.

Sombres ombrages, surpris d'un rayon de soleil!
On attend pour chanter. On accorde une lyre.
Est-ce la fin d'un monde ou son commencement.
Oh! il n'y aura plus de repos! tout s'étire!
De la terre qui naît, c'est l'ensemencement.

Éveillez-vous, belle endormie, qui tenez les clefs du bonheur,
Il existe un dieu qui ne parle qu'à l'aurore
C'est vous!
C'est vous, chère petite nature, grande
Terre. Oh! que le frais soleil nous rende
Les fleurs, vert Palais froid et doux.

Dawn

WHO awaits the Lord this pearly morning?
The moist black grass, the tree's mystery
All the groves are ready for consecrating.
The numbed foliage that the cold night nips.

Love lifts up the curtains of the night,
Love strews roses at the foot of the bed
The rose garden has been plundered.

The ocean is blond and round as a sky,
The sky is round as a berry.[46]

Sheltered shadows surprised by a ray of sun!
All wait to sing. A lyre is tuned.
Is it the end of a world or its beginning.
Oh! There will be no more rest! All is resumed!
Of the earth reborn it is the sowing.

Awaken, sleeping beauty, who hold the keys to happiness,
There is a god who speaks only at the dawn
It's you!
It's you, dear delicate flower, great
Earth. Oh! May the cool sun regenerate
The flowers, greenest Palace cold and sweet.

DEUXIÈME PARTIE

SECOND PART

Mélancolie du Sénéchal
La rivière est bordée en perles
L'homme était gai—ça m'est égal
Pour une femme d'âge et qui fait du cheval
Se peut-il qu'on se perde?
Rameaux, la mer, amour à mort
Remords.
Je reviens du pays d'où viennent les Péris
J'ai tissé les fils d'or et les bas de coton.
J'aime et c'est ma folie.
C'est ma folie d'aimer.
Régence, s'il eût pu, Sénéchal, qu'importune
Le clément souvenir de sa fortune
Au ventre dérobez les secrets de l'Atlas.

THE melancholy Seneschal
The river's edged with pearls
He was glad—I don't care at all
For an older gal who rides a horse
Is it possible to fall?
Boughs, waves, forever love and worse
Remorse.
I've returned from the land of the Peris[47]
I've spun golden thread and cotton stockings.
I love, it is my folly.
It is my folly to love.
Seneschal, were he able, regency
Pestered by his lost fortune's clemency
From the belly lift the Atlas' secrets.

Effet de lune

DES tiges de mourons!
Quelque insecte au chapiteau du mouron.
Et l'homme des bois de ces cathédrales
Tombant la tête en bas, ou rampant ou montant
Voit la lune à travers les fourches latérales.
Au bout des avenues de grelots de mouron
Il voit ton disque, ô lune! ô lune! œil de faucon,
La lune superbe et tisseuse de miel.
La lune superbe déborde le ciel,
La lune, œil d'oiseau et séjour des faunes,
Et reine de la flore et reine de la faune,
La lune superbe déborde le ciel.
Mais il est sur ses gardes, ô lune,
Car ce soir tu présides du haut de tes tribunes
A la fête que donne le miroir de l'étang,
L'étang, couleur de mouron.
Ah! les feuilles de rave, les tiges de mouron!

Moon Effect

STEMS of pimpernel!
Some insect in the big top of the pimpernel.
And the woodsman of these cathedrals
Falling head first, and crawling or climbing
Sees the moon through the fork's horizontals.
At ends of roads of bells of pimpernel
He sees your disk, oh moon! moon, falcon's eye,
The superb moon and weaver of honey.
The superb moon overflows the sky,
The moon, bird's eye and home to fauns,
Queen of flora, queen of fauna,
The superb moon overflows the sky.
But it is on its guard, oh moon,
For tonight you preside upon your court
At the party thrown by the mirror of the pond,
The pond the color of pimpernel.
Ah! the turnip leaves, the stems of pimpernel!

La guerre et la paix

BELEM ou Balaam, c'est de l'araméen
Préfère l'aramon, brigadier Larramée.
Tu partis! et Vénus qui te ceignit les reins
En fournira le scythe exil de nos armées.
Fleuri d'or, le hamac obturateur des branches,
Aux billes du soleil, laissons l'araméen
Il regonfle d'orgueil des hêtres le dimanche.
Or tempête! le vent accorde
Éole, de ton accordéon
Les cordes.
Pour l'aviatic d'Héligoland
Goéland
L'univers est en Daghestan
La mer, étang, l'étend
Par l'aviatic, aronde,
On se bat à la ronde
Mais un
Parait l'araméen
Jésus qui n'est plus de ce monde.

BELÉM or Balaam, it's in Aramaic
Wants aramon, brigadier Laramie.[48]
You left! And Venus who girded your loins
Scythian exile[49] endows on our army.
Gold-glowing hammock, branch-obturator,
To sunned logs let us leave Aramaic
Sundays it reinflates the beech trees' pride.
Now, storm! The wind tunes the chords
Aeolus,[50] of your accordion
The cords.
For the aviatic in Heligoland[51]
Seagull, land
The universe is in Dagestan[52]
The pond of the sea, spanned
By the aviatic, aronde,[53]
The fight's all around,
But one
Spoke Aramaic
Jesus, who's no longer around.

COMME un bateau le poète est âgé
Ainsi qu'un dahlia, le poème étagé
Dahlia! Dahlia que Dalila lia.

POÈME

Précipiter une aile à cette perle: un casque,
Pour atteindre le feu du ciel à son déclin
Et le serpent volait vers le Sud-Africain.
Deux dragons se battaient pour la victoire de Max
Au-dessus d'un couvent de moines turlupins.
Vingt champignons du bois ressemblaient aux marquises
Ayant ouvert leurs gros pieds blancs en pantalons
Oui! le ciel me connaît! il faut qu'on se le dise!
Mais il importe peu aux temps où nous vivons.
J'ai, lycéen, tutoyé mes professeurs
Ils m'apprenaient les dessins persans couleur bonbon
J'en ai gardé comme on garde des violettes
Quadrilles! j'ai dansé avec l'enfant de ma sœur
Déguisé sur mon épaule ou sur ma tête
Chez ma tante on avait mon lit dans le salon
Et je ne me levais qu'à midi au plus tard
Son fils lui reprochait le luxe de mes cigares
Voici le précipice où mon arbre a grandi
Il y a là un amphithéâtre de jeunes filles roses et blanches
Je me suis couché au bord et j'ai lu des livres
Mes jeunes pensées étaient en robe de dimanche
Elles avaient des fleurs dans leurs cheveux lisses.

A boat, the poet is a man of old
A dahlia, the poem's manifold
Dahlia! The dahlia Dalilah laced.

POEM

Upon this pearl precipitate a wing: a helm
To reach celestial fire at its decline
The South African drew the serpent's line
Of flight. Two dragons fought for Max's victory
Above a convent full of knaves divine.
The twenty wild mushrooms like marquises
Their fat stalks of open pantaloons are festive
The heavens know me, yes, hear its decrees!
Little may care the age in which we live.
In high school, I was pals with my professors
Who taught me candy-colored Persian sketches
Which I've kept as one might keep pressed flowers
Quadrilles! my sister's child was in stitches
A costumed dance upon my head or shoulders
My bed was made in the salon at auntie's
At most I would be out of bed by noon
His expensive cigars! her son would soon
complain. This precipice where my tree grew
Here there is an amphitheater of pink and white girls
I would sit on the edge and read books
In Sunday best my youthful thoughts wore dresses
With flowers in their long, straight tresses.

Je suis les évadés de la prison de Nantes
Un enfant reconnut notre tonsure au front
Quand nous lui demandions la route de Clisson
Les arbres, le soleil, le moulin, le torrent
Quand les nonnes servantes
Témoignaient devant Dieu pour leur déposition
Étaient un escalier de mon couvent de Nantes
Pour cacher l'infamie de ma vie de prison.

I followed prison fugitives from Nantes[54]
A child recognized our tonsured brow
When we asked him the way to Clisson[55]
The trees, the sun, the windmill, the torrent
When the nuns, servants
to bear witness to God in deposition
steps to lead me to my convent in Nantes
to hide the infamy that is my prison life.

Malachites

LES amis sont arrivés avec des figures allègres
Ils venaient du chemin de la montagne
Le chemin par où l'on apporte le bois de la montagne.
Il y a un petit noble de l'almanach Gotha
        Qui est nègre,
Un écrivain, un fonctionnaire et un danseur de l'Opéra
Ils se sont reflétés dans mes miroirs
Ils ont délibéré sur la maladie du danseur
Et lui ont conseillé le camphre et le phosphore.
Tous les six excepté le nègre
Nous avons mangé des cadavres
Avec du sel avec du poivre
Avec de l'huile et du vinaigre.
Le nègre ne mange que des fleurs cuites
Et les arrose d'eau bénite
Dans des bols.
Sous la vérandah de sable
De sable jaune et de cuscutes,
L'écrivain a joué de la flûte
Et il a évoqué le diable.

Malachites[56]

FRIENDS showed up with cheerful faces
And they were coming from the mountain trail
Wood is carried from the mountain on that trail.
A little nobleman from the *almanach de Gotha*[57]
    Is a negro,
A writer, a bureaucrat and a dancer from the Opera
Are all reflected in my mirrors
Deliberating on the dancer's illness
They suggested phosphorous and camphor.[58]
All six of us, except the negro
We all ate cadaver
With some salt and with some pepper
With some oil and some vinegar.
The negro only eats cooked flowers
He sprinkles holy water over
In bowls.
Beneath the sand of the veranda
With yellow sand and with cuscuta,[59]
The writer plays a flute, we revel
As he himself evokes the devil.

Écrit en 1904

L<small>E</small> tombeau de Pilate autant qu'il m'en souvienne
C'était à Draguignan si ce n'était à Vienne
Les fils d'Adb-el-Kader y prenaient des photos
Pour les suspendre au clair du clair en ex-votos
Les déesses filaient l'écume de la mer
Et pêchaient des disques d'or dans les étangs
Les laveuses frappaient les heures au passage
Et la Loire montrait son âme à tous les coins.
Mademoiselle Biscorne envahie par les eaux
L'abeille butinait un soleil puis un autre
Et ses ailes de feu couvrirent tout l'azur
Vif argent tenancier de Boukhara chambarde
L'ombre de l'ombre amie des lunes enchantées
Double-six! à moi la pause! disait-on.
Moi, j'ai les plus beaux bras, toi les plus beaux tétons
À nous deux nous ferions une femme parfaite.
Œuvre de Ducerceau le Pont-Neuf fait la roue
Les nymphes de la Seine à l'aube sur sa proue
Peignent leurs longs cheveux en chantant du Villon
La ville voyageait portant son âme en peine
Traînée par des hâleurs et par de lourdes chaînes
Les prêtres pélagiens venaient au devant d'elle
Les poissons suivaient l'ombre des chars anciens
Demande à son mari faire un tour de bateau
Le soleil du matin plume un arbre en poussière
Jésus barre la route entre les boulingrins
Le ciel est sur la terre pour qui veut bien le voir
Dans une maison du Straoumbourgenstrasse

Written in 1904

P ILATE's tomb as far as I can recall
   In Draguignan if it wasn't Bhopal[60]
The sons of Abdelkader[61] took some photos
To hang them up openly as ex-votos
The seafoam goddesses spun from the sea
And in ponds they would fish for golden discs
The washerwomen, they would strike the hours
And the Loire showed its soul to every corner.
Here's Miss Contort[62] overrun by the waters
The bee would browse a sun and then another
And its wings of fire covered the sky
Bukhara's[63] quicksilver tenant upturned
The shadow of shadows, magic moons' friend
Double six! My turn for a break! they said.
I've got the best arms, you the nicest breasts
Between us we'd make the perfect woman.
Pont Neuf, Du Cerceau's work,[64] does a cartwheel
Dawn's nymphs of the Seine, at its prow they kneel
Brush their long hair as they sing Villon's songs
The city traveled, its soul was in pain
Towed by haulers and by a heavy chain
The Pelagian priests went on before her[65]
Fish followed the shade old chariots cast
Asks her husband take a ride in a boat[66]
The morning sun, it plumes a tree with dust
Jesus blocks the road between bowling greens
Heaven is on earth for he who wants it
Inside a house on Straumbourgenstrasse[67]

—Tiens! les démons ont toujours les yeux bleus—
Sur une malle ainsi que dans une glace
Un poète mort jeune rasait son menton bleu.
Diana Castelucho, moteurs Gnômes et Rhône
Koto, vin de Coca des coteaux du Pérou
Avec la langue rouge du drapeau de velours
Grévistes les jupons jappaient sur les cailloux
Les ailes des pensées, pigeons que vous pensâtes
S'envolaient vers le sépulcre de Pilate.

Holà? nous déjeunons sur l'herbe
        Près de Marcajola
Et les roses nouées en gerbe
        À la ténorita

Robe en lanterne vénitienne.
        L'auto coupée en biseau
Chantons! recommençons l'antienne
        Pilate et son tombeau

La gueule des théâtres aux cinq mille œils des loges
Réfléchissait la mienne antienne ton éloge
Pilate. On grignotait la mandoline sous les toits
Et dans les restaurants on disait: « Le Roi boit! »
À célébrer Pilate nous nous exciterons
En buvant des « Amers » et des cocks au citron.
        Des deux atmosphères le ciel fait une marche
        Sur laquelle prophétisaient les patriarches

—What do you know, all demons are blue-eyed—
On a chest as well as in the mirror
A poet who died young shaves his blue chin.
Diana Castelucho, Gnôme et Rhône motors[68]
Koto, Coca wine of the hillsides of Peru
With the bright red tongue of the velvet flag
Workers on strike petticoats yapping on pebbles
The wings of your thoughts, pigeons you thought up
Took off toward the sepulcher of Pilate.

Holà? We have lunch on the grass[69]
     Near Marcajola[70]
And the roses tied in a bouquet
     For the tenorita[71]

Dress as Venetian lantern
     Car cut with a bevel
Sing! start again the antiphon
     Tomb of that Pilate devil

Theater's maw, five-thousand-eyeholed boxes
Which would reflect my antiphon your praise
Pilate. The mandolin was chewed on under roofs
And in restaurants they said: "The king drinks!"
Extolling Pilate's quite a jolly kick in
The pants! Sip the bitters with the lemon chicken.
     On these two moods shall heaven make remarks[72]
     From which came prophecies of patriarchs

Les marins blancs vêtus du bleu de l'Océan
De Pilate à Baal offraient le gant
Et la télépathie des radiotélégrammes
De Pilate partout faisait vénérer l'âme
Ceux de la politique et ceux de Théodose
Avaient aussi pris du Pilate à haute dose
Les Panthéons hémiplégiques depuis cent ans
S'émeuvent des éclairs et s'emplissent de sang.

The sailors dressed in white and ocean blue
Sent their glove from Pilate to Baal
The radiogram telepathy flew
That made all revere Pilate's soul
Those in politics and those of Theodosius[73]
These had also taken Pilate in high doses
The Pantheons, a hundred years half-paralyzed,
Fill up with blood: by lightning bolts they are surprised.

LES jurements aux dieux s'échauffaient de patois
Terrifiant les astres qui s'ajustaient en cônes.
Ricanais-tu, songeant aux châtiments des lois
Ô roi, sous le store noir peint des couleurs d'automne
Les arbres d'or voulaient sortir du bouquet de voiles
L'éclipse! bestial festin de roux avec les brunes!
Les terribles guerriers découpaient des gâteaux,
Dissimulant en eux les noirceurs de la lune!
Quand enfin la nuit vint, la nuit en clair de lune
Il n'y eut plus . . . Il n'y eut plus qu'un bord d'étang
La femme en vert qui peut-être était brune
Et l'enfant roux, l'enfant roux habillé de blanc.

THE oaths to the gods got hot with patois[74]
Scaring the stars that shifted into cones.
Did you snicker over sanctions of law
O king, beneath the awning's autumn tones
The golden trees wished to leave the veil bouquet
Eclipse! bestial feast of redheads with brunettes!
Terrible soldiers were cutting the cakes,
Hiding within themselves the moon's black nights!
When at last night came, the night in moonlight
There was no more . . . There was but a pond's edge
The woman in green who may have been brunette
And the redheaded child, the child clothed in white.

Thème de l'avantage des vertus

Enseigne: Au Syndicat des Rescapés de la Mouise
Mon petit parachute en peau de bégonia
Dans le même métal je fais aussi: chemise
Pastichant l'Alençon et le point d'Estérel
Chaussure sans pédoncule imitant le boa
C'est plus avantageux que la fibre de bois
Voiturette triplex avec paratonnerre de poche
Et double pédalier sur les côtés de la broche.

Enseigne: au Syndicat des Rescapés de l'Enfer
Non celui de la terre qui reçut cet ivrogne,
Jean-Marie Farina, marchand d'eau de Cologne
Le vrai, large et profond où pour punir les vices
Nous attendraient en bas de l'escalier de service
Satan et les employés de son service.

Entreprise de mécaniques agricoles
Cultivez les vertus dans les fermes-écoles.
Exhalaisons et salaisons en toutes saisons
Enseigne: Au Calicot de la Grande Espérance
Paris au Paradis par le Pari Mutuel
C'est celui de Pascal: Pari sauvez la France
Rendez Christ aux Larrons du juge au criminel
Enseigne: Au Blanc d'Espagne et de Madapolam
Par ordre du Préfet, recrépir sa pauvre âme.
Peindre le magasin à toute heure du jour
Et ne pas négliger la cour
Blanc! blanc! rata blanc

Theme of the Advantages of Virtue

PLACARD: Pickle Escapees' Union
My little parachute in begonia skin
Of that same metal I will make: a shirt
Pastiching Alençon and Estérel[75]
Shoe with no peduncle just like a viper
It flatters you more than any wood fiber
A triplex car with pocket lightning rod
Double pedal-and-gears on the sides of the shaft.[76]

Placard: Infernal Escapees' Union
Not that of the earth receiving this boozer
Jean-Marie Farina, a Cologne dealer[77]
The real one, huge, and where to punish vice
Would wait for us below the service stairs
Satan and all employees in his service.

Machinery for cultivating crops
In farm school cultivate the virtues.
Seasonings and reasonings in every season
Placard: At the Sign of Great Expectation
Paris in Paradise by Pari-Mutuel[78]
It's Pascal's: the wager save the nation[79]
Give Christ to Thieves from judge to criminal
Placard: In Spanish White and Madapollam[80]
On Prefect's orders, to reparge[81] one's soul.
To paint the store at all times of day
And the courtyard's not to be ignored
Blank! blank! drawing a blank[82]

Blanc partout, c'est le Bilan
De la Grande Maison de Blanc
Que le cri de mes jours perce l'airain des ciels.

All is whiteness, that's the score
At the Grande Maison de Blanc[83]
May my days' cry pierce through the heavens' steel.

PLUS qu'un hérisson blanc, recouvert de ses lances
Un fort de nacre avait ses couleuvrines blanches.
Un donjon où le soleil pointait
Et que jamais la bonne pluie n'adoucissait
Les soldats rouges en la cave fondaient des balles
Et roulaient des boulets en haut des vingt greniers
Et puis on s'exerçait au tir et de longs râles
Revenaient du ciel jaune, descendaient l'escalier.
Un fort de nacre! qu'on mit en sa poitrine
Car tout ceci n'est que folie que j'imagine
Pour dire ma tristesse et mes grandes douleurs
Causées par tant de gens au dur cœur
Et par tant de déboires et de leurres.

MORE than a white hedgehog covered in pins
A pearly fort had its white culverins.[84]
A keep that the sun shone upon
And never mellowed by the good rain
In the cellar red soldiers cast bullets
And rolled cannonballs in twenty garrets
And then target practice and some slow groans
Came back from yellow skies and slipped downstairs.
A pearly fort! put inside one's chest
For I've dreamed all this up as if in jest
To convey all my sorrow and my hurt
Inflicted by so many, hard of heart
And by so much illusion and defeat.

La rue Ravignan

à Dorival

Importuner mon Fils à l'heure où tout repose
Pour contempler un mal dont toi-même souris?
L'incendie est comme une rose
Ouverte sur la queue d'un paon gris.
Je vous dois tout, mes douleurs et mes joies . . .
J'ai tant pleuré pour être pardonné!
Cassez le tourniquet où je suis mis en cage!
Adieux, barreaux, nous partons vers le Nil;
Nous profitons d'un Sultan en voyage
Et des villas bâties avec du fil
L'orange et le citron tapisseraient la trame
Et les galériens ont des turbans au front.
Je suis mourant, mon souffle est sur les cimes!
Des émigrants j'écoute les chansons
Port de Marseille, ohé! la jolie ville,
Les jolies filles et les beaux amoureux!
Chacun ici est chaussé d'espadrilles:
La Tour de Pise et les marchands d'oignons.
Je te regrette, ô ma rue Ravignan!
De tes hauteurs qu'on appelle antipodes
Sur les pipeaux m'ont enseigné l'amour
Douces bergères et leurs riches atours
Venues ici pour nous montrer les modes.
L'une était folle; elle avait une bique
Avec des fleurs à ses cornes de Pan;
L'autre pour les refrains de nos fêtes bacchiques

Rue Ravignan

For Dorival[85]

BOTHERING my Son when all is in repose
To contemplate an evil that you mock?
The fire's like a rose
Open on the tail of a gray peacock.
I owe it all to you, both pains and joys . . .
I've wept so long for your forgiveness!
Break the turnstile that keeps me in a cage!
Iron bars, farewell, we're leaving for the Nile;
We take advantage of a Sultan's voyage
And of villas built with twine while
The orange and lemon would line the weft
And the galley-slaves wear turbans.
I'm dying and my breath is at the peaks!
I listen to the songs of emigrants
Port of Marseilles, ahoy! the lovely town,
The pretty girls, their handsome paramours!
In sneakers all the townsfolk run around:
Pisa's tower and the onion salesmen.
I miss you so, o my rue Ravignan!
From your heights they call antipodes
On pipes they taught me love, sweet shepherdesses
In their rich attire and their dresses
They've come here to show us the *dernières modes*.
One was crazy, she had a nanny goat,
With flowers in her horns of Pan;
The other for the chorus of our bacchanals

La vague et pure voix qu'eût rêvée Malibran.
L'impasse de Guelma a ses corrégidors
Et la rue Caulaincourt ses marchands de tableaux
Mais la rue Ravignan est celle que j'adore
Pour les cœurs enlacés de mes porte-drapeaux.
Là, taillant des dessins dans les perles que j'aime,
Mes défauts les plus grands furent ceux de mes poèmes.

A pure, vague voice, some dream of Malibran.[86]
The impasse de Guelma has its corregidors[87]
And rue Caulaincourt has many art dealers [88]
But as for me, I'm the one who adores
Rue Ravignan for the hearts my standard-bearers
Entwine. There, as I carved my pearl love-tokens
My greatest flaws were those of my poems.

L orsque l'empereur qui devait renoncer à la souveraineté
Reçut le message, il prenait le thé
Dans la chambre des femmes, près de son marcassin.
Il porta la main gauche au-dessus de son sein
Et prononça tout bas, avec beaucoup de zèle,
Des paroles embarrassées et immortelles:
« J'ai mal écrit les lois, il faut les arranger,
Voici qu'il est trop tard pour les changer! »
Les flammes du foyer étaient comme des griffes,
Le papier dans le feu tordait des logogriphes,
Et le vieux roi prit le chemin du monastère.
Cette retraite stupéfia l'univers.

WHEN the emperor who would give up sovereignty
        Received the message, he was taking tea
In the lady's chambers, near his baby boar.
Just above his breast his left hand he bore
And under his breath he said with great zeal
Words both awkward and immortal:
"My laws are bad, I must rearrange them,
Too late, I'm too late to ever change them!"
The flames of the hearth resembled vicious glyphs,
The burning papers turn to logogriphs,[89]
The old king to a monastery fled,
And over that the whole world lost its head.

Plus d'astrologie

ASTRES, vous combattez avec les seuls regards!
Des étoiles grouillaient comme un boisseau d'abeilles
Pendant ce long combat pas une qui sommeille
Eugénie Portefoin, le patron fait la bombe
N'entrez pas, Eugénie, le patron fait l'amour
Des filles, le patron faisait une hécatombe
Ma belle, n'entrez point, on n'en sort pas toujours

Astres, vous combattez avec des traces
Une larme tombait d'un astre
Ivre de joie je compulsai tous les trésors
L'éclat de la comète était vermeil
C'est moi seul qui l'entrevoyais dans mes veilles.
Ce sont les projecteurs qui forment les patries
Combats, nous combattons à l'ombre de nos sorts
Et le rouge de Mars est un rouge de mort
On a placé et déplacé trois diplomates
Dalila s'est donné pour maître un contremaître
Tous les hommes illustres décédés en quatre ans
Les notaires qui vendaient nos terres sont au camp.

Et l'œil du Christ ayant les clefs de mon logis
À jamais je renonce à toi, l'astrologie!
Vous, Quatre Couronnés, Sivère, Victorin, Séverin,
    Carpophore
Il fallait qu'il en fût ainsi! Prenez les clefs du coffre-fort!
Que pense le Seigneur notre Dieu des désastres
Que causent à ses amis les combats de ses astres.

No More Astrology

SPHERES, you do battle with your gaze alone!
Stars were teeming like a bushel of bees
All this long battle through not one who sleeps
Eugenia Portefoin, the boss is making merry
Don't go in, Eugenia, the boss is making love
Among the girls, the boss, he makes a killing
Don't go in, sweet thing, some never get free

Spheres, you do battle with your tracing
A tear fell from a star
Drunk with joy I pored the treasures over
The comet's shine was vermillion
As I stood vigil I alone could glimpse it.
These are the projectors that form the nations
Battles, we battle in the shadow of our fate
And the red of Mars is the red of death
Three diplomats have been appointed and displaced
For a man Dalilah chose a foreman
All famed men killed within four years[90]
The notaries that sold our land are in the camp.

And Christ's eye, having keys to my abode
I give you up for good, astrology![91]
You Four Crowned Martyrs, Severus, Victorinus, Severian,
    Carpophorus[92]
It had to be thus! Take the keys to the safe!
What thinks the Lord, the God of these disastrous ends
The battles of his spheres have wrought upon his friends.

Nous! chantons la petite baleine couleur cadavre
Chacun s'habille ici et les moins élégants,
Selon la fantaisie—silhouette choisie!—
De tableaux anciens et pour toute sa vie:
Barabbas, Sesostris, quelque Scythe, un brigand
Que Salvator Rosa peignit au bord d'un gavre
Nous! chantons la petite baleine couleur cadavre.
Au pied des grands Palais qui sont mappemondes d'astres
Plus de lumière à tels aquariums dévastés.
N'était la bave rouge lorsque ça ne rit plus
Les dorades déformées par la viande des victimes
Qu'on jette vivantes! (Justice soit au crime)
Ont tout le poivre et sel des cadavres perclus.
Monstres lourds! honorés comme on fait des bouddhas
Je vois tachés par archers, des vieillards las
Et dont ces aquariums géants seront les tombes.
Les dorades nageant vides de faims nouvelles
Désenchaînaient leurs traces et la piste éternelle
Fuyant les bonzes au loin et qui frappaient des gongs.

L ET us! sing the whale the color of cadaver
They're all dressed up, down to the least exquisite,
With all the fancy—the choicest silhouettes!—
of old paintings, throughout their lives, forever:
Barabbas, Sesostris, a Thracian, a pirate[93]
That Salvator Rosa[94] painted near a freshet
Let us! sing the whale the color of cadaver.
At the foot of Palaces which are star charts
No more light for such aquariums laid waste.
Were it not for red drool once the laughter's over
The breams deformed by the meat of victims
Thrown to them alive! (May justice be done)
Have all the salt and pepper of crippled cadavers.
Heavy monsters! honored as the buddhas are
I see archer-besmirched old men who are
weary; these vast aquariums will be their tombs.
The breams now emptied of the urge to feed
From this eternal track and from their pathways freed
Themselves and fled the monks still striking gongs.

Doit et avoir

Tracez une ligne de Liège à l'embouchure de la Bidassoa.
Tracez! tracez aussi la ligne de l'amour,
Côté "Doit," toute image de sérénité,
L'autre côté les plaisirs fous, la vanité,
De l'arche de Noé faites sortir les bêtes . . .
L'emphatique éléphant et le sinistre bouc,
Attendez la colombe au rameau d'olivier,
Renvoyez à Satan ce que vous lui devez.
Doit les chartes nouvelles à mon bon ange.
Au diable: l'inconstance, la surdi-mutité.
Sieur Fortuné du Bois Baudran,
Le gouverneur des Deux-Siciles
A fait, sur l'une de ces îles,
Faire un château de carton blanc.
Sol fatal! Solfatare! tare,
Du matin blanc jusques au soir
Il lui monte de ces Tartares,
Des visiteurs en habits noirs.
Doit le château à Dieu, la Sicile à l'enfer.

Debit and Credit

TRACE a line from Liège to the mouth of the Bidasoa.[95]
Trace! Trace as well the line of love,
Debit side, every image of serenity,
On the other mad pleasures, vanity,
From Noah's ark lead out the beasts . . .
Emphatic elephant and sinister goat,
Await the dove with the bough of olive,
Return to Satan that which you owe him.
To my good angel owe the new charter.
And to the devil: a fickle, deaf-mute nature.
Sir Fortuné du Bois Baudran,
The two Sicilies' governor,[96]
Had built on one of these islands
A white cardboard castle tower,
Fatal soil! Solfatare![97] tarry,
From white mornings to the evenings
There arise from this Tartarus[98]
Visitors in black wrappings.
Owe the castle to God, and Sicily to hell.

BERTRANDE a vu des phares roussir la nuit!
Tant que la Malaisie au collier d'or aura
des phares, ô Ciel, farci les corails verts
Tant que le monopole des navires d'aujourd'hui
Aura du monstre gigantesque, aura
déçu les rocs pervers
Bertrande, tu verras
les phares roussir la nuit.
Les lamas bicolores, les crocodiles cendrés
ricanent, mâchonnant des feuilles de papier
Moi, j'ai ma flûte où geindre
et ma barque où pleurer.

Korea

BERTRANDE has seen the beacons scorch the night!
As long as this Malaysia golden-necklaced has
lighthouses, Heaven, stuffed the corals green
As long as this monopoly of ships in sight
will have, of this gigantic monster, will have
let down the willful rocks
Bertrande, you will see
the beacons scorch the night.
Two-tone llamas, ashen crocodiles
snicker, chewing over paper files
As for me, I've got a flute on which to wail
and a bark in which to weep.

L ES trente-six ports! quels coteaux en couteaux
Les trente-six ports ont trente-six portes
    Et cent bateaux.
Les trente-six fraises sur le buis du buisson
Les trente-six fraises, c'est trente-six braises
    Et leur charbon
Trente-six veilleurs au congrès des veilleurs
Des chapeaux rouges en peau de chat
    Pour les meilleurs.
Les trente-six cors aux bois de l'Hellespont
Les trente-six cordes aux trente-six cors.
    Et leurs façons
Et tout le mal et les dures leçons
Qui de mon cœur ont fait un entrepont.

Thirty-six ports! what assorted moats
Thirty-six ports have thirty-six forts
    And hordes of boats.
Thirty-six faces on the knife-like knolls
Thirty-six faces are thirty-six blazes
    And all their coals.
Thirty-six sentries at the sentry-fest
And these red catskin hats for all
    Their very best.
Thirty-six horns in the fields of Carthage
Thirty-six cords adorn thirty-six horns.
    And their usage
And the hard lessons and evil thorns
That have made my heart a steerage.[99]

Le kamichi

L'ÉCHAFAUD, c'est la guillotine.
On n'en veut plus, c'est pour les rois!
L'humble auteur qui t'écrit ces lignes
Veut pour le moins mourir en croix
Je trempe mon roseau dans le sang de mon cœur:
     Titre ou dommage? animalcule
     Dieu vous trouvera ridicule!
     Allez donc vous faire pendre ailleurs!
     On vous accorde
     L'Asile de nuit et la corde.

La digitale étonne au bord des bois
J'en veux avoir autour de mon tombeau.
Fais un extrait de cette plante et bois,
Et tu seras guéri de tous tes maux.

Allons! découpez-moi un bon morceau de marbre
Avec dessus mon nom en lettres d'or;
Vous planterez auprès tel ou tel arbre
N'oubliez pas la date de ma mort

Je n'ai jamais pu être militaire
Étant moitié fil de fer et coton
Mais je fus dévoué aux compagnons,
Obstacle au bien que fait le monastère.

Ça sent la fraise! Ça sent la mandarine!
Juges-gardiens disent que le roi boit

THE gallows is the guillotine,
No more of that, it's just for kings!
The humble one who writes these things
Would like a cross to end his spleen.
I dip my reed in the blood of my heart:
> Title, damage? animalcule
> God will laugh at your ridicule!
> Now go hang yourself somewhere else!
> We'll give you the right
> To rope and a bed for the night.

Astounding foxgloves[101] by the woods would make
Good trim around my tombstone all in rows
Now make of it an extract, then partake,
And then you shall be healed of all your woes.

Go on! cut me a nice slab of marble
With my name in golden script upon it;
And beside it plant a shady arbor
And the day I died, don't you forget it

I never could be in the military
Being half of steel and half of butter
But all my friends were never treated better,
They block the way to a good monastery.

It smells like strawberries! It smells like tangerine!
Guard-judges say the king is on the sauce

Moi, Bourtibourg, je dis qu'on m'assassine
Juge, arrêtez! Je veux mourir en croix!

Acte d'amour que je mets par écrit:
Chacun son lot! Si j'ai le Saint-Esprit
Fors que mourir, je ne veux rien sur terre
Mourir, encor vivant de Sa Lumière.

I, Bourtibourg,[102] I say they'll do me in
Judge, stop! I want to die upon a cross!

This act of love to writing I commit:
To each his fate! If I have the Spirit
I desire naught but to die tonight
To die, and yet still living by His Light.

Périgal-nohor

ON a fait des reprises dans l'azur de mon ciel
    Deux lions s'accroupissaient à mes épithalames
Et sainte Catherine a relevé sa lame
Pour tailler mes buissons tressés couleur de miel—
Les deux châteaux pointus bourrelés de tourelles—
La tourelle au château avait des écrouelles.
C'est tout ce qui restait dans cette capitale
Et des bouts de jardin dispersés ça et là
Et nous voyions aussi vos coiffes de dentelle
Madame Adamensaur
Couleur de hareng-saur
Madame Mirabeau, Madame Mirabelle
Nabuchodonausaure, mère du roi, dit-elle.
Des voiliers revenaient vers cette cathédrale
L'un avait des trésors et l'autre du coaltar
Le troisième prit feu qui portait Abélard
Et la mer avait quelque chose de végétal
Et moi j'écris ceci en lettres capitales
Je ne serai jamais qu'un écolier dans l'art
Collier des écoliers nous portons des couronnes
Celui qui les reçoit vaut celui qui les donne.

SOMEONE's patched up the azure of my sky
My nuptials had two lions standing by
And then Saint Catherine[104] lifted her blade
To prune my honey-colored shrubs in braids—
Two castles on which little towers dwell—
The little castle tower's scrofules swell.
It's all that was left in this capitol
With bits of garden scattered here and there
And we could see your coifs of lace as well
Madame Adamunzipper
The color of kipper
Madame Mirabeau, Madame Mirabelle
Nebuchadnezzar's mother, truth to tell.
Now sailboats returned to this cathedral
One with gold and the other with coal tar
The third one catching fire carried Abelard[105]
While the sea seemed somewhat vegetal
I write in letters that are capital:
I'll never be but a novice in art
The novices' necklaces we wear crowns
The one who's crowned amounts to he who crowns.

GLACE d'idéal; tulipe au zénith
Et qui se flétrit et qui se dépite
Le pistil s'exaspère d'être pâle
Aurais-je aux nues offert le vide
La mère disait tout à la pauvre odalisque
Qui ne comprenait rien
Assise avec les rois au pied de l'obélisque
Et se mourait de faim
Adieu, pas effeuillés sur la neige mourante
Je vais me marier
Avec le duc d'Otrante
S'il veut bien m'accepter
Neige, il neige! elle aspire
À l'humecter, belle vierge de cire
Espère, futur, un ciel de fiel plus pur
Divulguez! l'extrême étage déifie la lumière
Choisis l'espace, tribune légère
Où la lumière peut voir l'ivoire de la lumière
Tige, exhausseras-tu le rêve où s'exténue
Cette âme si ténue.
Les astres faisaient des paysages en comète
Et les oiseaux nichaient dans les soleils mouvants
J'écrirai donc toujours mes vers sur mes manchettes
Ah! mes pauvres chansons, qu'à regret je regrette!
Le château de Chatou n'est qu'une escarpolette
Et j'ai laissé mes vivres à Montserrat.

GLASS of ideality; zenith tulip
And who wilts with pouting lip
The pistil is put out to be pallid
Would I have offered to the skies a void
Mom hid nothing from the poor odalisque
Who didn't understand
Sitting with kings beneath the obelisk
And was starving to death
Farewell, footprints plucked off in dying snow
I am going to wed
The Duke of Otranto[107]
If he'll have me she said
Snow, it's snowing! she breathes in
To melt it, lovely waxen virgin
Hope, future, for a sky of gall more pure
Divulge! the upper level deifies the light
Choose space, lighthearted tribune
Where light can see the ivory of light
Stem, will you raise up the dream where this slight
Soul grows exhausted.
The planets made some comet-landscapes
And birds nested in the suns' moving shapes
Ever on my cuffs shall I write my lines
Ah! my poor songs, that I to my regret regret!
Chatou's castle[108] is naught but a swing-set
And I left my victuals in Montserrat.[109]

L'INTRINSÈQUE satrape étrenna la pudeur des reines
Il égrène à des cryptes ses graines.
Ascète il définit la Ninive
Définitive
Les thèmes de l'œdème qu'il aime
—À jamais aimer!—
Admets Atrophialcus au tiers conseil des princes
Paladin obscurci par un hymen secret
Il refuse de joindre au duché trois provinces
Qu'un pape libéral à ses filles offrait.
Il ne s'enrichit point et vieillit dans ses fautes
Comme un ermite à qui tout était étranger.

THE intrinsic satrap tried the modesty of queens[110]
In crypts enumerates his grains
This ascetic knows the definition of a
Definitive Nineveh
Lovable he deems the themes of an edema[111]
—to love forever!—
Now let Atrophialcus[112] counsel princes
This paladin obscured by secret hymen
A liberal pope has granted him a token
Land offered to his daughters: he refuses.
He never grew rich, he grew old in sin
As though a hermit from the world estranged.

Plaintes d'un prisonnier

PERCHEZ les prisons sur les collines
Nous aurons la respiration saline
Ça nous consolera de la discipline
Barbe-Bleue est ici depuis une huitaine
Avec ses beaux-frères, avec Croquemitaine

« Anne, ma sœur, ne vois-tu rien venir
Regarde la mer bleue, regarde l'avenir!
—Je ne vois que l'aumônier et le médecin
Ils arrivent dans le bois de pins
Et leur aspect
Me rend perplexe et circonspect
Faut-il me donner la fièvre jaune
En me frottant le nez avec la paume
Ou une fluxion de poitrine
En buvant mon urine. »
La fille du geôlier et le récidiviste
Des résultats du steeple ont consulté la liste
Comme près des colonnes il y avait du vent
Ils ne lurent pas plus avant
Et la belle a fait un enfant.
Un entomologiste qui est sous les verrous
Étudie à son gré la punaise et le poux;
Nous avons un préfet, un notaire, un abbé,
Les malheureux, ça n'est pas bête,
Ont fait de la cloison un piano alphabet
Ils se disent tout ce qui passe par la tête.
—Moi, je n'ai jamais pu l'apprendre—

A Prisoner's Complaints

PERCH the prisons on the hills
  We'll have saline respiration
From discipline some consolation
Eight days Bluebeard's stay has spanned
With brothers-in-law and the Bogeyman

"Anne, my sister, do you see anyone?[113]
Watch the blue sea, watch what's to come!"
"I only see the chaplain and the doctor
They're coming to the pinewoods
And their aspect
Leaves me perplexed and circumspect
Should I give myself the yellow fever
By rubbing my nose with my finger
Or give myself pneumonia
By drinking my urine."[114]
The jailer's daughter and the recidivist
For steeplechase results they consulted the list
Since it was windy near the columns
They didn't read any further
And the lady was made a mother.
Under lock and key an entomologist
Studies to his heart's content the bedbugs and the lice
We've got a prefect, a notary, an abbot,
The poor devils, it's not so dumb, I find,
Made the partition an alphabet piano,
They tell each other all that comes to mind.
—Me, I've never had the hang of it—

D'hommes à femmes des choses tendres.
Prisons, volière des doigts muets
La muse est un oiseau qui passe
Par les barreaux de ma prison
J'ai vu son sourire et sa grâce
Mais n'ai pu suivre son sillon.

Adieu, muse, va dire aux hommes
Ce soir de fête en la cité
Que dans les prisons où nous sommes
On meurt de les avoir aimés.

From men to women, the sweet nothings bit.
Prisons, aviary of mute fingers
The muse is a bird going by
Straight through the bars of my prison
I've seen her smile and her grace
But I could never keep her pace.

Farewell, muse, go tell the men
While the party's on again
That in prisons where we lie
For having loved them, we die.

L E cerf de bois venu de la nuit
La nuit pâlie d'un horizon très proche,
Ses yeux n'étaient que crasse et sur le buis
Le cerf de buis sur une roche,
Il ne broutait que le bois de la nuit
Le râtelier d'herbe en bois et puis!
Puis l'herbe s'enflamma brune comme les loches:
C'était comme au théâtre une rampe Auer
La nuit était toujours la nuit
Et le cerf affamé broutait l'herbe d'enfer.

COME from the night the buck out of wood
Close horizon of a night pale as bone,
Its eyes were foul and in boxwood
The boxwood buck upon a stone,
Grazing nothing but the night's wood
The grassy wooden rake and then would
Then would the grass burn brown as loaches:[115]
Thus the theater's Auer ramp[116] approaches
The night was the night still
And the starving buck would graze the grass of Hell.

Pastiche

Avez-vous rencontré la fille au muguet bleu
Qui m'aime sans me vouloir?

Avez-vous rencontré le lièvre au poil de feu
Qui broute à mes réfectoires?

Avez-vous rencontré le vieillard chassieux
Qui dit non sans rien savoir?

Avez-vous rencontré pucelle aux jours heureux
Qui a différé l'écart?

Avez-vous rencontré gueux devenu plus gueux
Qui a voulu trop avoir?

Avez-vous rencontré malin malicieux
Qui lance ferraille et pétard?

Avez-vous rencontré puissant officieux
A savant quêtant savoir?

Avez-vous, tout compte fait, avez-vous gobé les œufs
Venant de mon poulet noir?

HAVE you met the flower-laden miss
who loves but doesn't want me?

Have you met the fiery puss
as it grazes my refectory?

Have you met a rheumy ignoramus
refusing gifts unwittingly?

Have you met the maiden who in joyous
days deferred the splits protractedly?

Have you met the increasingly monstrous
goon who hoarded far too greedily?

Have you met the rogue who's mischievous,
launching cherry bombs with glee?

Have you met the lord who sought the service
of men in wisdom's company?

Have you, now won't you tell us,
my black hen's eggs: have you sucked any?

Thème de l'illusion et de l'amour ▬▬▬

LES chiens d'un certain Actéon
　Ne dévoreront pas leur maître:
Ils le feraient des vagabonds.

Existence paradoxale que le clair de lune fait naître,
Sur les pelouses du château!
Non! ce ne sont pas des joyaux
Sur les chiens et les paillassons
Mais des gouttelettes du jet d'eau.

Le danseur:—un zeste de citron—
Poursuit Diane au jeu de cache-cache
Les fenêtres qu'on dépassa l'éclairaient en grêle malgache.

Ilote! oh! maigre lot! les pompes du soleil!
Pour donner aux oiseaux le signal de l'éveil
Voici la lune! sors donc en ouvrant ton ombrelle
De ce muscat, raisin en clocher de chapelle.
Le masque de Basile était un masque nègre
Blanc, le côté d'amour! l'autre côté vinaigre.

Theme of Love and Illusion ═══════════

THE dogs of one named Acteon[118]
Will not their master devour
But they might eat some vagabond.

Paradoxical existence that the moonlight begets,
Upon the castle's lawns so green!
No! It is not of jewels, that sheen
Upon the dogs and the doormats
But the fountain's tiny droplets.

The dancer:—a lemon zest—
Pursues Diana, hide-and-seek
From windows we leaned out of, shined upon in Malagasy
    sleet.[119]

Helot![120] oh! meagre lot! Sumptuous sun!
To give birds the signal to awaken
The moon! Come open up your umbrel
From this Muscat, grape as belfry of a chapel.
Basile's[121] mask was African, love's half
White as flour! the other half was sour.

LES minutes sonnaient comme un timbre d'argent
La lingère étendait au loin des linges blancs
« Voici l'heure du rendez-vous!
Chantait le chœur dans la coulisse
—Ce pantalon est à coulisse
Se disait Triboulet le fou.
Avec un sucrier d'argent,
Qui de pomme faisait l'office
Aux cannes d'un bonnet à poil, le fou blanchissait un merlan
—Mes six enfants sont en nourrice.
—Ils ne sauraient être moins mal.
Et les autos légers bougeaient au moindre vent.
Triboulet offrait tout pour avoir la lingère
Il saupoudrait le linge et sucrait les merlans
Mais le soir qu'elle faiblit le fou lui dit:—Va-t'en
—Quoi, disait Triboulet, on prend l'une après l'une. »
Il s'en alla jouer du clairon sur la dune
Et les petits marins penchés sur les goélettes
Croyaient entendre au loin Neptune et sa trompette.

LIKE a silver chime the minutes rang out
Far off the laundress's linens spread out
"It's the hour of the rendezvous!"
 Sang the choir in the coulisse
"This waistband's a coulisse"
 Said Triboulet the fool to himself.[122]
 With a silver sucrier
 Which acted as a pommel
 For the canes of a bearskin hat, the fool parboiled a whiting
"My six children have a nanny"
"They could hardly be better off."
 The light cars shifted in the slightest wind.
 Triboulet gave it all up for the laundress
 He sprinkled laundry, sweetened whitings
 But the night she grew weak the fool said: "Begone"
"What? said the fool, you take 'em one by one."
 He went to play the bugle on the dunes
 And little sailors on the schooners stooping
 Believed that far off trumpet Neptune's.

Allusions romantiques à propos du Mardi-Gras ▬

Non, Monsieur Gambetta, Bolivar est parti
Nous avons vu son tube et son aérolithe
Sous le jet d'eau des becs Auer
Pierrot cascade et compagnon.
Trahison blouse au coin du quai
Ce soir je dîne à la maison.
La Seine a vu passer les rois qu'on guillotine.
L'horreur des nuits te guette aux impasses gothiques
Ta selle, ô bicyclette, est un masque en velours.
Le vent d'Est animait les loges de l'Amour.
Adieu! s'il faut mourir, Madame, écoutez-moi.
Les jupes et les cœurs descendaient jusqu'à terre
Et pour boire on levait un peu l'auriculaire
Ma vie est un tango, mon cœur un mélodrame
Le destin! halo de peur à Notre-Dame!
Fleuret! c'est un fleuret, non c'est une badine
Pardonnez-lui, Gérald, au nom de notre amour
Je ne veux plus de vos caresses
Ah! quand sortiras-tu des bagnes de l'amour.
Les femmes s'offraient comme de jeunes chiens.
Parfois, la Seine est infernale après minuit.
Allons! Monsieur de Belzébuth, je vous provoque.
Dégainons! je vous brise comme un œuf à la coque
Il faut que l'un de nous débarrasse le monde.
Il dit! puis ce fut l'immense ennui sans profil des nuits sans
lune.

Romantic Allusions Concerning Mardi-Gras ▬▬

No, Gambetta, sir, Bolívar has left[123]
We've seen his tube and his aerolith too[124]
Under water-jets of Welsbach burners[125]
Pierrot[126] performs stunts with companion.
Platform corner treachery overalls
Tonight I dine at home.
The Seine has seen the kings they guillotine.
Nights' horror watches from gothic dead ends
O bicycle, your seat's a velvet mask.
The East Wind emcees Love's theater box.
Adieu! If I must die, Madame, then listen.
The skirts and hearts descended to the ground
To drink we wagged our ring finger round
My life's a tango and my heart a drama
Fate! Halo of fear upon Notre-Dame!
Foil! It's a foil, no, it's a switch
Forgive him, Gerald, for our love's sake
I want no more of your caresses
When will you leave the hard labor of love.
The women gave themselves up like young dogs.
Sometimes the Seine is hellish after midnight.
Come on, Beelzebub, I'm egging you on.
Draw! I crack you like a soft-boiled egg
The world is too small for the both of us,
Says he! then it was the immense, featureless ennui of nights
      without the moon.

Paysage

Nous autres, signons les papiers
Pendant qu'ils visiteront l'atelier
Le capitaine de marine dont la jambe bat la cloche
Arrive avec un bouquet d'aristoloches
Ma mère est affligée du mariage
À cause de la différence d'âge
Combien l'horizon, l'horizon des arbres
Est balafré; poussière de blés! rayons de sabres!
Pour se morfondre en conjectures
Sur notre ménage futur
Une vieille offre un miroir au vent
Et fixe des constellations sur le divan
Son cadeau de noces est
Un coffret de coquillages violets.
Les charrettes à malles autour de la maison
Commencent à rôder avec leurs monstrueuses cargaisons
Autour de la maison dans les vignes de la cour.
Il pleure dans tes bras
O ma fiancée, l'enfant de nos amours
Déjà!
La femme du matamore pour être spirituelle
Se déguise avec des fleurs artificielles.

Landscape

Let's sign the papers, hurry up
While they're visiting the workshop
The marine captain's here with his wandering leg, to pay
His respects with a birthwort[127] bouquet
My mother's distressed about the marriage
Due to the difference in age
How the trees, the trees' horizon's
Hewn and scarred; wheat dust! sabers' beacons!
To dwell upon conjecture
Of our happy household's future
Raising mirrors for the wind to blow upon
A hag charts the stars on a divan
Her wedding gift's a set
Of purple seashells in a small casket
The carts of luggage awfully close to home
Hauling their monstrous cargoes have begun to roam
Close to home in the garden vines today.
In your arms he swoons
It's our lovechild oh my fiancée
So soon!
Just to be witty the Matamore's[128] wife spends hours
Dressing up in artificial flowers.

Vous avez inventé que deux et deux font quatre
      Votre mariage est fondé là-dessus
Je suis veuf et je crois au canard à trois pattes
      Pas de danger d'être cocu.

Mais cuissons à ma peau fut deux et deux font quatre
D'antidote antidate on dit mithridaté
L'être ose m'en vanter, non de l'avoir été
      Pousse tard la troisième patte

Je veux, sangles à bœuf, mon Dieu, je veux ta grâce
Effort! sois couronné! Dieu, qui m'y faites asseoir
« Dites! qu'y gagnez-vous?—Je ne suis pas rapace.
On demande un petit miroir. »

Bouche arabique à ta philosophie, ô Gange!
Il gave un péritoine ailé, celui de l'ange.
Il s'amuse, oublié en quelque Moravie,
Des jeux divers d'un mot ravi.

Sers d'un patient effort Apollon Musagète
      Sois bien avec les anges
Car ces juges sont de ceux que notre muse achète
      Par des chants de louanges

Le Paradis, s'il vous plait.
Au poète enfant de paix
Le Pilori des enfers

So you've invented two and two make four[129]
You built your marriage on it—my wife's no more
And I believe in a bee with three knees
    Zero risk of cuckoldries.

Yet tan my hide did two and two make four
Call antedate antidote mithridated[130]
Being thus I boast, not having been before
    The third knee is belated

I wish, girth dimwit, God, I want your grace
Effort, be crowned! God, you sit me pretty
"Say, what's in it for you?"—"I'm not greedy.
    Set a mirror in this place."

Arabian mouth to your mind, oh Ganges!
He stuffs a peritoneum,[131] the angel's.
He's amused, forgotten in assorted
Lands, by the word transported.

With patience serve Apollo muses' leader
    Follow angels' ways
These are judges whom our muse can flatter
    With our songs of praise

Paradise, if you please.
For poets born of peace
The Pillory of hell

Pour ta bonne et ton tailleur
Que tous ces gens batailleurs
S'aillent faire battre ailleurs.

For your maids and tailors
All these vulgar squabblers
Can take a hike as well.

L ES beaux jambages que la mer écrit! et c'est
Et c'est pour toujours, pour toujours effacé,
Rien qu'un message et puis on rentre
On rentre, brouff! se battre le ventre—
La mer—comme l'eau d'un évier
Sans qu'aucun rocher rose ait pu la dévier.
La corvette a touché le ras des polypiers.
Va! rivalise à la course, ô lambeau de mer amère!
Des enfers la mer lance l'écume
Rivalise avec le soleil qui becquète le ciel vert
La corvette a touché, ô mer, les mystérieux polypiers
Mer! ah! que l'équipage est las de la manœuvre
Mer! offre ta feuille pure, tel un papier,
Aux galets en fête que tu ne peux charrier
La machine a des cris, les bras vains d'une pieuvre
Et trois vieux marins s'apprêtent à recuire
Le goéland mourant dont la chair est si dure
Ainsi quand mon esprit, etc. . . .

WHAT fine downstrokes written by the sea! No doubt
No doubt forever, forever blotted out,
Just a word and we'll be off again
We'll be off, baroom! to rack our brain—
The sea—a sink full of water
No rosy reef has ever made to falter.
Against the polypary runs the cutter.
Come join the race, oh bitter tatters of the sea!
From hell the sea will hurl its sea spray
Vie with the sun grazing a sky green as can be
The cutter's touched the polypary's mystery
Oh sea, ah! of work the crew are weary
Sea! your purity's a slip of paper
To please the pebbles that you cannot carry
Shrieks escape the engine, the useless arms of squid
And three old sailors overcook the dreaded
dying seagull's flesh as tough as leather
Even so does my mind, etc. . . .

L E renard au corbeau demande son fromage
Pour l'homme toute femme est d'abord un corbeau
Donc, ne soyez pas si fière de nos hommages
Le canapé des dieux est le même au bordeau.

Les habits tirés au cordeau
Et cette moustache en cordage!
Darwin assigne au paon les buts d'un tel plumage.

Il se peut qu'un moine astique
Des madrigaux sans ferveur
Cette exception monastique
En l'étant se donne tort.

Moi j'ai la main clouée au disque de la lune,
Éclaboussez, ô sang, les étoiles du ciel
Des anges, savez-vous, qui font les clairs de lune
L'un broda mon esprit avec de l'irréel,
Pour me descendre vers vous Dieu fit une échelle
Je ne suis pas assez long
Il y manque un échelon
Prêtez-moi vos ailes.

THE crow's cheese the fox would love to pillage[132]
Now to men women are first of all crows
So, do not be too proud of our homage
The gods' couch is the same in bordellos.

With these perfectly tidy clothes
And this moustache all of cordage!
To peacocks Darwin fixes goals for such a plumage.

Perhaps a monk may fashion
Madrigals tepidly sung
This monastic exception
Being one admits to wrong.

My hand is nailed to the disk of the moon
Oh my blood, splatter the stars of heaven
The Angels who make the light of the moon
By one of these was my spirit woven
To lower me to you God's ladder swings
I'm too short by a hair
A rung is missing there
Lend me your wings.

Invocation-vocation

LES plis des voiles sont des rimes
Or ceux de l'eau se désarriment
Les noms sortent en capitales
Sur les maisons des capitales
Et s'y collent c'est la réclame
Des nobles et fortes maisons
C'est aussi celle de nos âmes
Peintres chassés du Panthéon
Ô Muse, printemps spirituel
Par cette nuit de décembre
Ce n'est pas selon le rituel
Que je vous invoque en ma chambre.
Votre voyage sur la terre
Fait éclore des fleurs dans les serres
Il a fait rêver le marin
Qui voit vos pieds blancs sur l'embrun.
Ô m'approcher de ton lampadaire électrique
Muse! relever tes cheveux, Électre
Le rythme, l'endormir dans le sable du ciel.
Puis l'étaler aux pieds des dieux en arc-en-ciel
Ô! calme pensionnat des Muses à la lueur fumeuse des Étoiles.

Invocation-Vocation

THE folds of all the sails are rhymes,
At sea they come unmoored at times
The names come out in capitals
On houses of the capitols
And stick—they're that publicity
A noble house relies upon
As does our souls' felicity
Painters sacked by the Pantheon[133]
Oh Muse, spring so spiritual
Upon this cold December night
It's not as per the ritual
That I invoke you here tonight.
Your voyage over all the earth
Can bring the hothouse blossoms forth
For you the sailor's dreams will stray
Who sees your white feet in the spray.
O to come near to your electric lamp
Muse! To lift up your hair, Electra[134]
Rhythm, to send it to sleep in celestial sand.
Then spread it before the gods in a rainbow
O! calm boarding school of the Muses in the smoky light of
    Stars.

Atlantide

Entr'ouvre un continent plus jeune:
Nous aurons Ève après Bellone!
Un nouveau paysage sort de l'Océan:
Aux rochers pas encor de mousse
La première goutte de source
N'a pas encore mouillé le champ.
Un géant sur le haut de la tour Eiffel
—La lune est dans sa chevelure—
Rejette les enfants qui lui viennent du ciel
Afin de peupler la nature.
La tour du port, la nuit léchée par la tempête
C'est une corbeille de langues frisées
C'est tressé et la vague apporte ici les têtes
Des Èves pâles qui ont l'air de fuir.
On prépare le nouveau continent au Sacré-Cœur.
Un jeune homme a montré le modèle des maisons
Sur une estacade et les mains de Notre-Seigneur
Près de mon lit là-haut où sont les pèlerins en toute saison.
Il y en a qui se font des œufs sur le plat avec une lampe à alcool
Il y a un qui n'a que sa poitrine et son épaule
Il y a une paysanne bretonne.
Et le jeune homme est encore près de moi
Notre-Seigneur est nu dans le dortoir
Il donne ses mains percées
Le nouveau continent est une affaire de travail et de pensée
Et c'est au Sacré-Cœur que ça doit se passer.

Atlantis

Divide a younger continent:
We'll have Eve after Bellona![135]
A new landscape emerges from the waves:
On boulders no moss has yet grown
The very first drop from these springs
Has not yet moistened the meadow.
A giant on top of the Eiffel tower
—The moon is in his flowing hair—
Rejects the children the sky gives to him
To populate nature.
The port tower, the night groomed by the storm
It's a basket of curly tongues
It's braided and the wave brings the heads
Of the pale Eves with flighty airs.
The new continent is being prepared for Sacré-Cœur
A young man has shown the model of the houses
On a boom and the hands of Our Lord
Near my bed up there where the pilgrims are in all seasons.
There are those who make fried eggs with a spirit lamp[136]
There's one who has only his chest and his shoulder
There's a Breton peasant-woman.
And the young man is still near me
Our Lord is naked in the dormitory
He is giving his pierced hands
The new continent is a question of work and thought
And it must come to pass in the Sacré-Cœur.

Léon! Léon!

LA paille dans les forêts bruit de pas
Mon gros cousin dans une chambre
Expliquez-moi! expliquez-moi!
Je n'ai pas le courage de mettre l'autre soulier.
Il n'y a de véritables adieux qu'en prison.
Dans les étoiles je vois des couronnes
Et des auréoles apocalyptiques pour des lièvres uraniens
Le feu dans le poêle de fonte hurle à la mort
Léon! Léon! c'est comme ça tous les soirs
Pattes de l'horloge supplices de mouches
Troupes dans les maisons, les pauvres, seuls dans les rues
Je planterai un clou dans ta main bras du fauteuil
Un clou dans l'autre main du fauteuil
Des clous dans tes pieds de plancher
Et je te frapperai impératrice Eudoxie.
Je ne peux pas vous empêcher
Est-ce qu'il pleut?
Les anges télégraphistes ont des casquettes bleu pâle.
Averroès! est-ce un héros? un héros est-ce Averroès?
Comment colorer ma faiblesse
Moi qui suis un homme au courant
Si ce n'est par ce mot charmant
Délicatesse!

Léon! Léon!¹³⁷

THE hay in the woods the noise of footsteps
 My fat cousin in a bedroom
Explain it to me! Explain it to me!
I don't have the courage to put on the other slipper.
There are true farewells only in prison.
In the stars I see crowns
And apocalyptic haloes for Uranian hares[138]
The fire in the cast-iron pan howls up
Leon! Leon! it's like that every night
Legs of clocks flies' torment
Troops in houses, poor people, alone in the streets
I'll plant a nail in your armrest hand
A nail in the other hand of the armchair
Nails in your floorboard feet
And I'll strike you empress Eudoxia.[139]
I can't keep you from it
Is it raining?
The angelic telegraph operators have pale blue helmets.
Averroes! is he a hero? a hero is Averroes?[140]
How can I color my weakness
As a man who knows what's what
If not by that charming word
Sensitivity!

À la chaudière!

Toi, marchande animée, défiante, très affable
  Ton voyage aux amygdales de l'enfer
Pour des motifs dont plusieurs sont inavouables
(Rappelle-toi l'artilleur du 24 juillet dernier).
Mécanicien tourneur entrée des modèles.
Veuillez voir à la caisse mademoiselle Adèle
L'idéal ris de veau pour lequel tu fautas
Te condamne à la circoncision posthume par téléphone
Chef ou cheffesse! tes fesses bues par le nitre
Tu cours oh! ne cours plus après le ris de veau
Écorchement posthume du petit porc, Adèle!
Veuillez voir à la caisse; boîte de Mortadelle
Pieds truffés! brûlés vifs pendant l'Éternité
Mis en tisane, en boîte, en persil, en séné.
Là pas d'œil à monsieur le directeur de la Série
Pas de promesse à l'entrepreneur de la Scierie
Pas de frisure pour le Second de la Maison
Pas de protection du fils de la Maison.
Effroyable opération des vertèbres lombaires
On vous descendra dans les amygdales de l'Enfer.
Quoi! la plus belle, Adèle, à la Poubelle!
Le sort des femmes n'est pas douteux.
Ils ne sont pas bien frais vos œufs!
Arrête! il y a des arêtes à l'arrêt!
Je suis une personne honnête
Gare au fleuret pour qui me conterait fleurette
C'est bien! c'est bon! allez! madame Adam.
Mais prenez garde à vos dentelles

L IVELY saleslady, defiant, quite affable
Your trip to the tonsils of Hell
For various reasons, some dishonorable
(Remember the gunner from last July 24th).
Metal-turning mechanic input for models.
Please see the front desk Miss Adele
The ideal sweetbread for which you erred
Condemns you to posthumous circumcision by telephone
Boss or bosslady! Your backside absorbed by nitre[142]
You run oh! stop chasing the sweetbread
Posthumous flaying of the little pig, Adele!
Please see the cashier; box of Mortadella[143]
Pig's trotters! burned alive for all Eternity
Put in herbal tea, canned, with parsley, with senna.[144]
There, no eyes for the Series director
No vow for the sawmill entrepreneur
No perm for the Second-in-Command
No protection from the owner's son.
Horrifying operation on the lumbar vertebrae
You'll fall into the tonsils of Hell.
What! the prettiest, Adele, in the trash she fell!
Women's fate cannot be doubted.
Your eggs are hardly fresh!
Stop short! shortstops at a bus stop!
I'm an honest sop
Watch out! my foil foils the flirt
That's well! and good! go on, Madame Adam.
But watch your fishnet

Le porte-monnaie de Satan
Est en peau de lombes femelle.

For Satan's wallet
Is made of ladies' sacral hide.

Aux astres descendu, lui que baisa la Muse
Les degrés du zodiaque abreuvent ses loisirs
Verbe équipé d'émail noir sur de la céruse
Le chiffre en son obscur grenier l'a fait moisir
Tu sais que la Voisin, la Locuste moderne
Attira Montespan, les dames de la cour.
Un abbé défroqué dit la messe aux lanternes
Pour dérober au roi le fruit de ses amours
Toi, bateleur, très ennuyé du doctorat,
Satan s'adresse à toi par la pluie et le vent
Prends ta corde à la lucarne, ô rat
Et te pends aux dépens de la philosophie
La cour en notre temps goûte peu les sofis
N'espère pas la cour au carreau de ce temple
Il faut à nos autos un garage plus ample
Que ta mansarde. Et ta philosophie! ô fi!
Donc, bateleur, très ennuyé du doctorat
Satan s'adresse à toi par le vent et la pluie
Prends ta corde, dit-il, à ta lucarne, ô rat
Et te pends pour avoir trahi la poésie!

To the planets fallen, kissed by the Muse
These zodiac degrees his leisures nourish
A black-enameled verb upon ceruse[145]
The number in his attic made him languish
La Voisin, that Locust of the modern,
Met ladies of the court like Montespan.[146]
A defrocked abbot says a mass to lanterns
To rob the king of what his love begat
The doctorate has miffed you, acrobat,
Satan calls to you through the rain and wind
So to the dormer take your rope, o rat
And hang yourself to spite philosophies
The court today is hardly fond of Sufis
And so expect no court to grace this temple
Floor: our cars seek carports far more ample
Than your loft. Fie to your philosophy!
The doctorate has miffed you, acrobat,
Satan calls to you through the rain and wind
So to the dormer take your rope, o rat
And hang for thus betraying poetry!

La Mort

PHILATÉLISTE, ombre et soleil
  Degrés! bout de bottine.
L'ombre et la tête du lézard
Voyant le triomphal retour boulevard Malesherbes.
Non la pointue girouette efface
Laine les ongles.
Son nom pas encor dans le dictionnaire
Bout de bicorne académique.
Portail.

Death

PHILATELIST, shade and sunlight
Degrees! bit of a bottine.[147]
The shadow and head of the lizard
Seeing the triumphant return boulevard Malesherbes.[148]
No the pointed vane erases
Nap the fingernails.
His name not yet in the dictionary
Bit of an academic bicorne.
Gateway.

TROISIÈME PARTIE

THIRD PART

MADAME la Dauphine
Fine, fine, fine, fine, fine, fine
Fine, fine, fine, fine.
Ne verra pas, ne verra pas le beau film
Qu'on y a fait tirer
—Les vers du nez—
Car on l'a mené en terre avec son premier-né
En terre et à Nanterre
Où elle est enterrée.

Quand un paysan de la Chine
Shin, Shin, Shin, Shin, Shin, Shin,
Veut avoir des primeurs
—Fruits mûrs—
Il va chez l'imprimeur
Ou bien chez sa voisine
Shin, Shin, Shin, Shin.
Tous les paysans de la Chine
Les avaient épiés
Pour leur mettre des bottines
Tine! tine!
Ils leur coupent les pieds.

M. le comte d'Artois
Est monté sur le toit
Faire un compte d'ardoise
Toi, toi, toi, toi,
Et voir par la lunette

MADAME Adeline,
Line, line, line, line, line, line
Line, line, line, line.
Will never see, will never see the pretty scene
In the film they made
—in the shade—
For she was buried with her firstborn
she was buried in Bourne
in a grave she was laid.

When a lout from the steppe
Step, step, step, step, step, step.
Wants the best loot
—Fresh fruit—
He asks the recruit
Or his friend the galoot
Step, step, step, step, step, step,
All the louts from the steppe
They saw them afoot
To give them the boot
Toot! Toot!
They cut off their foot.

Mr. Robert Surcouf
Climbed on the roof
To look for some proof
Goof, goof, goof, goof,
And to see with spyglasses

Nette! nette! pour voir si la lune est
Plus grosse que le doigt.
Un vapeur et sa cargaison
Son, son, son, son, son, son,
Ont échoué contre la maison.
Son, son, son, son,
Chipons de la graisse d'oie
Doye, doye, doye,
Pour en faire des canons.

Lasses! Lasses! if the moon passes
Through forefinger and thumb.
A steamer and its cargo come
Dum, dum, dum, dum, dum, dum
And crash against a home.
Dum, dum, dum, dum
Let's pinch us some goose fat
Cat, cat, cat,
To shoot our cannons at.

Villonelle

Dɪs-moi quelle fut la chanson
Que chantaient les belles sirènes
Pour faire pencher des trirèmes
Les Grecs qui lâchaient l'aviron.

Achille qui prit Troie, dit-on,
Dans un cheval bourré de son
Achille fut grand capitaine
Or, il fut pris par des chansons
Que chantaient des vierges hellènes
Dis-moi, Vénus, je t'en supplie
Ce qu'était cette mélodie

Un prisonnier dans sa prison
En fit une en Tripolitaine
Et si belle que sans rançon
On le rendit à sa marraine
Qui pleurait contre la cloison

Nausicaa à la fontaine
Pénélope en tissant la laine
Zeuxis peignant sur les maisons
Ont chanté la faridondaine! . . .
Et les chansons des échansons?
Échos d'échos des longues plaines
Et les chansons des émigrants!
Où sont les refrains d'autres temps
Que l'on a chanté tant et tant?

Villonelle[149]

TELL me what was that song that all
The sirens sang and made to lean
From the decks of every trireme
The Greeks who every oar let fall.

Achilles who took Troy, they say,
In a big horse all stuffed with hay
Achilles was a splendid captain
Though he was taken by the songs
The lovely virgin Hellenes sang
So tell me, Venus, hear my plea
Reveal to me that melody

Tripolitania's prisoner[150]
In prison he made yet another
So lovely that no price at all
Was demanded from his godmother
Who had been weeping at the wall

Nausicaa at the fountain
Penelope weaving her wool
Zeuxis upon houses painting[151]
Well, they all sang bibbledibull! . . .
As for the cupbearer's couplets?
Long echos of echos of plains
And of the songs of emigrants!
And where are all the old refrains
That were chanted strain upon strain?

Où sont les filles aux belles dents
Qui l'amour par les chants retiennent?
Et mes chansons? qu'il m'en souvienne!

And where have the young ladies gone
Held fast by the love songs men sing?
As for my songs? Well, let me think![152]

Réflexion d'un auteur inédit ▬▬▬▬▬

Office: Travail facile à faire chez soi.

Ah! qu'on me le vende à l'encan
Tout ce que mon cerveau découpe
Au lieu d'en écailler mon sang
Je le porterais en chaloupe.

Je suis facile à satisfaire
Ce devant quoi passe mon temps
—Dit la clientèle à Figuière—
Sans escompte on paie en sortant.

« Quoi! tant d'idées en un roman!
Dit un auteur qui désespère
—Chez notre grand apocrisiaire
On t'imprime et mieux on te vend! »

Drame à signer pour millionnaire
Ou simples sonnets pour amant
Si tu n'as pas assez d'argent
L'éditeur en fait son affaire.

Et moi qui huilais ma machine
Moi qui taillais dans mon cerveau
Des bas-reliefs, des hauts-fourneaux
Qui peignais comme on peint en Chine.

Reflections of an Unpublished Author

Bureau: Easy to do at home

Ah! Let them auction it all off
Like every cut my brain will butcher
I won't scrape my blood for the stuff
Instead I'd load it on a cutter.

I'm easy going, laissez-faire
I pass the time I write about
—Says the clientele at Figuière[153]—
You'll pay full price when you check out.

"All those ideas in just one book!"
Says the beneficiary
That the apocrisiary[154]
Prints and sells by hook or by crook!

Drama the millionaire will sign
Sonnets for a lover's sickness
If it's money for which you pine
Well, that's the publisher's business.

And me, I oiled my machine
I cut some chunks out of my brain
For smelting, or to carve a scene
I painted as they paint in Spain.[155]

Rien qu'une course en fiacre à faire.
—Ah! j'ai justement votre affaire.
Un vaudeville! six cents francs
Payables à tempérament.

I've just got an errand to do.
"Have I got an offer for you!
A vaudeville! a modest expense
You can pay it in installments."

Véritable petit orchestre ▬▬▬▬▬

(PARTIE DESCRIPTIVE)

Houlettes du Grésivaudan
Sur le sol glacé des prairies
Les souliers mordorés près des fleuves
Rochers ou les barquettes des bergers.

(PARTIE MUSICALE)

Saint sein! vive le rein!
Vive le vin divin du Rhin
Où Chio? ou Ténédo? louez l'Ohio.
Point! Point! Point!
L'auto miaule, pioupiou piaule
Marabout l'allume
L'allume à la lune.
Je vais faire la niche
La niche aux péniches
Point! Point! Point!
Bout des coussins des marsouins.
Point! Point! Point!
Pape! papal! pape alors à l'or.
Élie! Allah! Alain!
Tiens! il neige! zut.
Le rat pose beaucoup de plumes.

Authentic Little Orchestra ━━━━━━

CROOKS of Grésivaudan[156]
Upon the prairies' icy ground
The golden shoes near the rivers
Boulders or the tubs of shepherds.

(MUSICAL PART)

Blessed breast! Long live livers!
Long live divine Rhine's vines
Where's Chios? Tenedos?[157] Hail Ohio.
Not! Not! Not!
The limo mewls, puling pioupiou[158]
Marabout[159] moans
Moans at the moon.
I'm gonna make the wherries[160]
The wherries unwary
Not! Not! Not!
Porpoise brink of the squabs.
Not! Not! Not!
Pope! papal! papal laurel aura.
Eli! Allah! Alain![161]
Hey! It's snowing! drat.
The rat deposits many feathers.

Unanime j'aime et rôde
Nature sous la neige imperturbable
L'habitude du danger rend les hommes prudents et les femmes
    téméraires.

(PHILOSOPHICAL PART)

Unanimous I love and prowl
Nature under the imperturbable snow
Being used to danger makes men more prudent and women
reckless.

Musique acidulée

Boum! Dame! Amsterdam.
Barège n'est pas Baume-les-Dames!
Papa n'est pas là!
L'ipéca du rat n'est pas du chocolat.
Gros lot du Congo? oh! le beau Limpopo!
Port du mort, il sort de l'or (*bis*).
Clair de mer de verre de terre
Rage, mage, déménage
Du fromage où tu nages
Papa n'est pas là.
L'ipéca du Maradjah de Nepala.
Pipi, j'ai envie
Hi! faut y l'dire ici.
Vrai? Vrai?

Boom! Dam! Amsterdam.
Bombay is not Ramagundam![162]
Pappy will be back!
That's no sweet snack, that's rat's ipecac.[163]
Bingo of the Congo? Bravo, Limpopo![164]
The cold hold, it told of gold (*bis*).
Maid in shade inlaid in jade
Rage, mage, disengage
From fondue wars you wage
Pappy will be back.
That's the Maharadjah's ipecac.
Peepee, I really gotta
Hee! shout it out I oughtta.
Right? Right?

À mon beau-frère

DES jours passés à te traduire, Épitomé . . .
  Cinq heures! le piano! romance de Thomé!
Le dîner grave et lent: « Es-tu content de toi?
« Il ne le criera pas, mon père, sur le toit
Qu'il m'a griffé la langue et m'a mordu la manche
—Tu seras privé d'automobile dimanche!
Mordre sa sœur encore à treize ans! à cet âge! »
Et le collégien pleurait dans son fromage.

Beau frère! tu verras sous toi grandir ton fils
Sois tendre! la raison trouve toujours son fil
Mais c'est dans la bonté que le vrai jette l'ancre
Apprenons à aimer pour nous apprendre à vaincre.
Mon père du pardon avait tant l'habitude
Que son être au pardon empruntait l'attitude.
Sois indulgent, beau frère, et quand de chambre en chambre
Ton jeune fils poursuivra la femme de chambre,
Grâce pour les ardeurs de Robert mon filleul
Au nom du souvenir clément de son aïeul.
Et toi, lecteur! pardonne-moi, triste apprenti,
Si la musique et l'art par mes vers sont trahis.
Poète de trente ans, le cygne de ma lyre
M'ensemence de blanc sans que je sache écrire.

To My Brother-in-Law[165]

TRANSLATING you for days, Epitome . . .[166]
Five o'clock! Piano! Ballad by Thomé![167]
A solemn meal: "Happy with yourself, now?"
"Father, he won't shout from the rooftops how
He scratched up my tongue and bit through my blouse"
"No car this Sunday, you're stuck in the house!
Biting your sister at twelve, at your age!"
And so the schoolboy wept in his porridge.

Brother! As you watch him grow your son needs
Tenderness! Reason always finds its lead
But it's in goodness that the truth drops anchor
We learn to love if we would learn to conquer.
My father showed forgiveness so unsparing
His very being took forgiveness' bearing.
Brother, show forbearance, and when your son
The chambermaid from room to room shall run,
Grace for the passions of my godson Robert[168]
In honor of his forebear's clement heart.
And you, reader! Forgive this wretched novice
If this to art and music do disservice.
My thirty years the lyre's cygnet white
Seed sows in me, and still I cannot write.

Le testament de la biche

QUELLE forêt, poudre de rose!
Le ciel est couleur de vin blanc.
Et sur le ciel vin blanc se pose
Chaque branche comme un cheveu.
C'est comme s'il n'y avait jamais eu de vent.
Comme si tout était parent
Fille ou neveu.
Comme si les arbres montaient à cheval frère à frère
Ainsi sur une estrade les vaches se font traire.
Et aussi comme si avec des chiffres de millions
On faisait difficilement une division
Ainsi vont les arbres feuillus, roses dans l'air.
Aubade! Aubade! ô faon né du flanc de la mère
La biche est morte en te mettant sur terre
Et tes yeux, deux boules de jais, des yeux de verre
Sont moins émerveillés par la forêt en l'air
Que par la patte agonisante
Qui se pose sur un papier à lettres.
Le papier à en-tête de la maman
« Ceci! ceci est! ceci est mon testament. »

WHAT a forest, powder of roses!
  The sky is the hue of white wine.
Upon the white wine sky reposes
Each branch just like a hair.
It's as if there never had been any wind.
As if everything was kin
Daughter or nephew.
As if the trees rode horses cheek by jowl
Thus on a platform they would milk the cows.
And also as if with numbers in millions
It was hard to make any divisions
Thus go leafy trees, rosy in the air.
Aubade! Aubade![169] o fawn born from a mother's loins
The doe has died to bring you forth
And your eyes, two balls of jet, eyes of glass
Are less amazed by the forest in air
Than by the leg in agony
Alighting on letter paper.
The letterhead belongs to the mother
"This! this is! this is my will and testament."

Métamorphose absurde

L A gourde en osier comme mille fleurs jaunes et le gobelet
Où est le vin, sang du Christ.
La gourde en osier changée en valise
La poche en osier qui s'envolera
La poche en osier pointue des deux bouts
Elle s'envole et ne tient pas debout.
Voici la terrasse, balcon rue Saint-Denis
Le marchand: bazar, filets à papillons
Boîtes à pétrole, tout sur le balcon.
Passe l'aviateur dedans la valise
Il est enfermé dans la grande gourde
« Ouvrez-moi! ouvrez!—D'où venez-vous donc?
—Comme caporal je partis en guerre,
Je partis en guerre. Je suis général!
—Vous avez crevé ces filets à papillons,
Vous avez dérangé ma batterie de cuisine,
Il y a trois cents francs de réparations! »

Absurd Metamorphosis

T HE wicker gourd like a thousand yellow flowers and the cup
In which there is wine, blood of Christ.
The wicker gourd changed into a suitcase
The wicker pocket that will fly away
The wicker pocket pointed at both ends
Flies away and won't stay right side up.
Here's the terrace, balcony rue Saint-Denis
The merchant: bazaar, butterfly nets
Petrol canisters, all on the balcony.
Here comes the aviator in the suitcase
Within the big gourd he's all bottled up
"Let me out! open up!" "where do you come from?"
"As a corporal I went to war,
I went to war. I am a general!"
"You tore up these butterfly nets,
You made a mess of all my kitchenware,
That's three hundred francs to repair!"

La Sultane exilée

DIADÈME des tilleuls! les platanes maussades oh!
Les tilleuls! oh!
Les sureaux
L'orchestre de Hongrois—mazurke et varsovienne—
Fier du Sénégalais qui rit à la persienne
Redouble, s'alanguit, pleure et redouble encore
La femme du sultan prisonnier de Lahore
Est en villégiature à Royat du Mont-Dore.
Ordre de nos gouvernants
Pour attirer les Musulmans
Matari, c'est ainsi qu'on nomme l'exilée
Des sultans de Lahore portera la livrée
La sultane est bien triste
Elle envie les touristes
Ne pouvoir avec l'amant des casinos
S'égarer dans le bois pour chasser les moineaux
Sans laisser des lambeaux étoilés de ses pagnes
Aux orties des chemins, aux ronces des campagnes
Mais la reine arriva la reine du Congo
Et ce lui fut une compagne.

The Sultana in Exile

L INDEN diadems! the gloomy planetrees oh!
The lindens! oh!
The elderberry
The orchestra of Hungarians—mazurka and varsoviana[170]—
Proud of the Senegalese man who laughs through the blinds
Redoubling, languishing, weeping and redoubling again
The wife of the sultan who is prisoner of Lahore[171]
Is on vacation at Royat in Mont-Dore.[172]
On the orders of those governing us
To attract Muslims
Matari[173] is her name, she's in exile
Lahore's sultans, she'll dress in their style;
The sultana is downcast
She envies the tourist
Being unable, with a lover from casinos
To get lost in the woods chasing sparrows
Without leaving starry shreds of her skirts
In roadside nettles, brambled countryside
But the queen arrived the queen of Congo
And she stayed by her side.

L A colline de l'Occident est fraîche et pure
Merci à vous qui m'avez regardé avec confiance
Mon char de guerre, hélas! est un char d'ambulance
Et mes tambours sont détendus par la souffrance
La colline de l'Occident est fraîche et pure.

Mes règlements de tir sont flétris par les larmes
Mes bronzes sont fêlés par les mauvais serments
Oui! mes pleurs ont rouillé, rouillé mes belles armes.
Ah! je te voue à l'ombre des lunes
Royaume des batailles! . . . si tu n'étais plus! . . .

—Les floraisons parfumées n'attirent pas le petit oiseau vert
—La colline de l'Occident est fraîche et pure
Allons laver nos linges et vendre nos charpentes
La cigale est morte il faut la manger.
Je n'aurai plus dans l'âme que des articles de vente.
Je sors de l'Océan vermeil comme un fruit mûr
Les floraisons parfumées n'attirent plus le petit oiseau vert.

Un soir d'orage
Si chaud, si lourd, si sage
Ah! va, malgré ta glose et tes airs de combat
Tu n'as que l'air des tout petits enfants qu'on bat.

THE hill in the West is both cool and pure
   My thanks to you who have trusted in me
Alas my war machine's an ambulance
And my drums have grown slack from affliction
The hill in the West is both cool and pure.

Tears wither away my rules of shooting
The bronze has split from all my unkept vows
My tears have rusted my beautiful guns.
Ah! I damn you to the shadows of moons
Kingdom of battles! . . . if you were no more! . . .

—Scented blooms don't draw the little green bird
—The hill in the West is both cool and pure
 Let's wash our laundry, leave our bones for sale
 The cicada's dead it must be eaten.
 My soul shall contain nothing but retail.
 I leave the Ocean red as a ripe fruit
 Scented blooms no longer draw the little green bird.

One stormy evening
So hot, so stifling, so genteel
Ah! go on, explain, and stick out your lip
You've just got the look of toddlers they whip.

LES floraisons parfumées n'attirent plus le petit oiseau vert
La colline de l'Occident est fraîche et pure
    Madame ma mère, madame ma mère
    Du vaisseau amiral, j'aperçois la bannière.
Il n'avait pas achevé ses études
Qu'il était édenté comme le bord d'une étuve
    Madame ma mère, madame ma mère
    Donnez-moi votre main
    Je me suis trompé de chemin.
Trois sous dans une écuelle qu'il avait à la main
Il avait des mains de couturière
Enflées et pareilles à des pierres
Il avait une figure de rougeole
Des yeux qui clignent et qui volent.
    Le voici sur une selle doublée d'étamine
    Son cheval a bonne mine.
Madame ma mère, les nuages nocturnes sont avancés
Le brouillard se dissipe avec des trous d'acier
Sur la selle est un homard qui broie
La doublure de son pardessus de soie
Les floraisons parfumées n'attirent plus le petit oiseau vert.

II

S CENTED blooms no longer draw the little green bird
The hill in the West is both cool and pure
   Mother dear, dearest mother
   From the admiral's ship I see the banner.
Study wasn't over for him
Yet he was toothless as an oven's rim
   Mother dear, dearest mother
   Give me your hand
   To take the wrong path was unplanned.
Three sous in a saucer he held in his hand
He had the hands of a seamstress
Swollen and just like stones
He had a measles face
Eyes that wink and rove.
   Here he is on a saddle lined in bunting
   His horse looks in good trim.
Mother dear, the night clouds are nearing
Pierced by steel the fog is lifting
Upon the saddle is a lobster shredding
The lining of his silk overcoat
Scented blooms no longer draw the little green bird.

Voici l'ancienne ingénue
Au nez carré tout au bout
Arbres et monts sur les nues
Deux chiens courent après nous.

Sa fille qu'elle veut vendre
N'est que bonne et non pas entre
Cour et jardin. Dites-moi
Comme on présente au bourgeois
La mère? Fille-mère? la fille?
La mère? comme fille-mère? la mère?
La fille comme fille ou mère?

Certain docteur morphinomane
Chauve et vraiment comme il faut
Apprend à ces quadrumanes
Les secrets qui rendent beau

Un tramway mène à la montagne
Ceci se passe à la campagne.
Les deux chiens domestiqués
Quand ils seront astiqués

Ils vaudront bien deux mille.
Le docteur est un vicieux.
Pitié pour la Madeleine, mais
Non pour les avaricieux.

HERE's the former ingénue
Whose nose is square at the tip
On clouds, trees and mountains grew
After us two dogs will skip

She'd like to sell her daughter
Who's nothing but a housemaid,
And hardly posh. How ought her
Mother be mentioned? Unwed
Mother? As for the daughter?
Mother? As unwed? The mother?
Daughter as unwed or mother?

A certain addict doctor
Was bald and truly proper
He taught these quadrumanes[174]
Their beauty to maintain

A tramway to the mountain leads
It happens in the countryside
The two dogs of the tamest breeds
Once all their polish is applied

Will be worth a good two thousand.
But the doctor's full of vices.
Pity for the Madeleine,[175] and
Not for misers and their prices.

Il pleurait sur son infortune
Il désirait avoir la lune
Il pleurait et disait: « Hélas!
Si l'on savait comme je suis las. »

Tandis qu'à chercher sa pantoufle
Le gros fils du gros roi s'essouffle.
J'aime le Christ et je le prie
De l'aimer pendant cette vie.

Je veux que des esprits nouveaux
Adorent enfin mon plumage
Et qu'ils dorent d'un beau nuage
Les ailes de ma tête de veau.

H<small>E</small> wept upon his misfortune
And even wished to own the moon
He wept and said, "Ah! woe is me!
How weary I am, can't you see."

And as he will hunt for his slipper
The son of the fat king will whimper.
I love Jesus Christ and I pray
To love him for all of my days.

I want all the *esprits nouveaux*[176]
To worship my plumage out loud
To gild with a beautiful cloud
The wings of my *tête de veau.*[177]

SOMMEIL! soleil! prends les persiennes
Le tapis rouge éteint les pas
Tu peux dormir jusqu'à ce qu'ils viennent.
Le canapé de la princesse étend son velours incarnat
Giramor dit: « J'ai vu votre doux fils, madame!
    —Où donc?
—La chair en fleur de Cupidon!
Il se roulait sur votre malle
Il avait baudrier, c'était une guirlande
Point d'arc, l'air naïf et mutin
Puis là, sur le dossier, à portée de la main
Il s'allongea comme une offrande.
Pendant que vous parliez
Il admirait votre sourire perlier
Je l'ai vu qui jouait avec vos cheveux noirs.
Le prince dit: « Moi, je le sais dans la maison
Vous avez donc les yeux de l'esprit pour le voir
Cupidon nuptial est notre compagnon
Tandis que le Bottin professe
Le divorce de nos altesses. »

SLUMBER! sun! take up the blinds
The red carpet mutes the footsteps
You can sleep till they arrive.
The princess' sofa spreads out its rosy velvet
Giramor[178] says, "I saw your sweet son, Madame!"
    "Where?"
"Cupid's flesh in bloom!
He rolled upon your trunk
He bore a sling, it was a wreath
No bow, a naïve and impish air
And there, against the backrest, within reach
He stretched out like an offering.
As you were talking for awhile
He admired your pearly smile
I saw him playing with your black hair.
The prince says, "I know he's in the house
So you have soul enough to see him
Nuptial Cupid's our companion
While every phonebook entry
Lists some divorce among our gentry.'"

La marâtre moderne

L E cimetière ne voudra plus d'elle
Que moi, le vieux, j'en voudrais encore
Elle souhaite ma mort
Pour ne plus me voir!
Elle dit qu'elle fera jeter mon corps à la voirie
Sans mentir
Oui! sans m'enterrer!
L'aîné de mes garçons me disait: « Père, attends
Que nous t'ayons quitté avec nos vingt ans
Pour prendre en légitime cette femme interlope
Cette ancienne donzelle, ce despote! »
Ma seconde femme veut qu'on soit amoureux d'elle!
Elle n'était pas plutôt entrée dans le logis
Qu'elle excitait le plus petit!
L'enfant fit sa malle pour le pays berbère
Afin de résister à sa seconde mère!
Alors ce fut l'aîné qu'elle enragea
Lui, dans les aviateurs militaires, s'engagea.
Elle me trompe chez mon cocher
Sa main bat plus que son cœur: un rocher.
Et moi je la regarde avec couardise
Sans penser même à lui donner un coup hardi.

The Modern Wicked Stepmother

THE cemetery won't want her anymore
While I, the old man, want her still more
She wants me dead
To see no more of me!
She says she'll have my body thrown in the street
It's no lie
Yes! without burying me!
The eldest of my boys said to me: "Father, wait
Until we leave at twenty, and on that date
You may wed that former sexpot,
That shady dame, that despot!"
My second wife wishes to be loved!
She had hardly entered the house
And already she'd aroused the youngest!
The child packed his bags for Berber country
To resist his second mother!
The eldest she riled up later
He enlisted as a military aviator.
She's cheating with the coachman
Her hand beats more than her heart: a stone.
And I watch her like a cowardly slug
And hardly think to dole out a good slug.

Petite ville anglaise le dimanche ▬▬▬

à Georges Gabory

S ur l'antique fronton d'un antique bazar
On s'avise d'un nom *Company Balthazar.*
Sur la glace des rues glissent des messieurs veufs,
Les trottoirs rasés de la veille sont neufs.
On regrette que les enfants ne soient pas blonds le dimanche
On les trempe dans la farine par la jambe ou par la manche,
On en blesse certains dans la chevelure
On y mêle des doigts de pied
Jusque dans la figure
Les mères sont pareilles à des tulipiers
Et leurs demoiselles pareilles à des tulipes.
Les vaisseaux pavoisés battent de l'aile au port
Je n'ai plus de passion si ce n'est pour la pipe
(Ce n'est pas vrai!)
Auberge de ce jour où l'eau même s'endort
Ton spleen hyperbolique
Me rendrait alcoolique.
Nul marin sur les mâts dont les croix sont des tiges
Aux dames escogriffes ne donne le vertige.
Moi d'abord: triste échalas
Qui fais étalage de cet état là,
Le ciel en cône, bocal, prison des anges!
Ô mes rêves! glissez au sommet des fleurettes.
Châteaux décrits, écrits, arcs-en-ciel d'insectes,
De ma tête dans l'herbe le regard oblique vous guette!
Lambris, nombrils, verdure

Little English Town on Sunday

For Georges Gabory[179]

On the ancient facade of an ancient bazaar
The name can be seen there, *Company Balthazar.*[180]
On icy streets slide widowers of late,
The sidewalks freshly shaven, up to date.
Too bad they're not blond on Sundays, these children we
      perceive
They're dipped in flour by the leg or by the sleeve,
Sometimes their hair is injured
Toes are mixed in
Right in the face
Their mothers are like tulip trees
Their young misses just like tulips.
Bedecked their vessels flap their wings in port
Besides the pipe I have no more passions
(That's not true!)
Inn of this day when even water dozes off
Your spleen is hyperbolic
It'll make me alcoholic.
At the mast where the stems of crosses grow
No sailor gives the twiggy ladies vertigo.
Me for starters: on a roll
In the sad role of beanpole,
The sky in a cone, bell jar, angels' prison!
O dreams of mine! slide to little flowers' summits.
Castles described, inscribed, insect rainbows,
Head in the grass, my oblique gaze surveys you!

Où la terre met le nez dans sa fourrure
Teints du sang du soleil c'est celui de mon cœur.
Le frêle florentin de la carte postale
Porte au cœur un tambour qui bat la générale
Mais moi le receveur des impôts indirects
J'ai la tête un dimanche au niveau des insectes
Le soleil incendie ma nappe de chemise
Ce matin j'ai prié trois heures à l'église
Est-ce que je dors ou si je veille
Il y a un violon quelque part
Trois arbres qui voudraient danser, la mer approche son oreille
Moi j'ai le ciel bleu pour miroir.
C'est la cour de Marie qui le tient à deux mains
Des prophètes, des rois, des saints clairs et des anges
La méridienne, Greenwich et sous ton méridien
Donnez-nous aujourd'hui notre pain quotidien.

Paneled walls, navels, green pasture
Where the earth puts its nose in its fur
All dyed with blood of the sun, my heart's blood.
The slight Florentine in the postcard
Sounds the alarm with the drum in his heart
But me the collector of indirect taxes
This Sunday my head is at the insects' axis
The sun ignites the surface of my shirt
This morning I prayed three hours in church
Am I sleeping or if I'm awake
There's a violin somewhere
Three trees that would like to dance, the sea approaches its ear
As for me, the blue sky's my mirror.
The court of Mary holds it in two hands
Prophets and kings, and bright saints and angels
Under Greenwich meridian, meridian[181] in bed
Give us this day our daily bread.

Invitation au voyage

à Louis Bergerot

Les trains! Les trains par les tunnels étreints
Ont fait de ces cabarets roses
Où les tziganes vont leur train
Les tziganes aux valses roses
Des îles chastes de boulingrins.

Il passe sur automobiles
Il passe de fragile rentières
Comme sacs à loto mobiles.
Vers des parcs aux doux ombrages
Je t'invite ma chère Élise.
Élise! je t'invite au voyage
Vers ces palais de Venise.

Pour cueillir des fleurs aux rameaux
Nous déposerons nos vélos
Devant les armures hostiles
Des grillages modern-style
Nous déposerons nos machines
Pour les décorer d'aubépine
Nous regarderons couler l'eau
En buvant des menthes à l'eau.

Peut-être que sexagénaires
Nous suivrons un jour ces rivières
Dans d'écarlates automates

Invitation to a Voyage[182]

For Louis Bergerot[183]

Trains! Trains by the tunnels constrained
Have made of these cabarets' pink
Where gypsies come and entertain
The gypsies with their waltzes pink
Of islands chaste with bowling greens.

They pass by in automobiles
The brittle heiresses pass by
Like a lot o' moolah on wheels.
Toward the parkland's gentle umbrage
I invite you, dearest Alice
I invite you on a voyage
Toward those palaces of Venice.

To gather flowers from the bough
We'll set aside our bikes for now
Against the armored and the hostile
Cast-iron grates in modern style
To one side we'll set our machines
To drape in hawthorn white and green
We'll watch the water flowing by
As we sip our iced teas and sigh.

Perhaps when we're sixty moreover
We'll travel down many a river
In scarlet-red automatons

Dont nous serons propriétaires!
Mais en ces avenirs trop lents
Les chevaux des Panhard
Ne seront-ils volants?

À vendre: quatre véritables déserts
À proximité du chemin de fer,
S'adresser au propriétaire-notaire
    M. Chocarneau,
    18, boulevard Carnot.

Écrit en 1903

And we ourselves will be their owners!
But in these long-awaited futures
The Panhard[184] cars, their horses
Won't they all know how to fly?

For sale: a desert vacation
Quite nearby the railway station
Write to the owner's location
      Monsieur Chocarneau,
      18, boulevard Carnot.

Written in 1903[185]

Fête

L'ORDRE de l'arc-en-ciel pour décorer la nuit
Palais en diamants de vertèbres lombaires
J'étais à bord de son étage empli de fête
Et les femmes montraient à table leur ennui.
Il y en avait cinq parées comme des serres
Dont les yeux noirs brillaient regrettant le dessert
Et pour chaque arrivant elles tournaient la tête.
La terrasse était couleur de feu d'artifice
Et pleine de danseurs, de duellistes de feu.
Dans les chambres étaient des divans somptueux
Où des gens déguisés attendaient l'impossible
Les Indous s'incarnent des pierres dans la peau
Il n'y a pas mieux qu'eux pour la bonne aventure.
« Montrez vos ongles!—Hélas! ils ne sont pas très beaux!
Et les lignes des mains sont d'un triste futur. »
Ailleurs on dansait la danse des ongles sans remuer
Et les mains oscillaient comme des étoiles.
Je dis à la sibylle: « Vous êtes une merveille!
Vous m'avez énuméré mes peines à merveille. »
Deux héros de Balzac à dos de batraciens
Qui passaient dans mon dos quand on lisait ma main,
Me dirent: « Dans ton lit, tu n'y toucherais pas! »

Gala

T<small>HE</small> rainbow's order decorates the night
    Diamond palace of lumbar vertebrae
Here I was aboard its gala-filled floor
And the dining ladies showed they were bored.
Five of them were bejeweled as hothouses
Their black eyes would shine regretting dessert
With each arrival they'd swivel their heads.
A patio the shade of fireworks
And full of dancers, duelists of flame.
Inside the rooms were sumptuous divans
Where masks awaited the impossible
Hindus set gemstones right into their skin
They're the best there is at fortune-telling.
"Show me your nails!—Alas! they're not so nice!
Your hands show the lines of a fate so bleak."
Elsewhere the fingernail dance was danced without moving
And all the hands swayed back and forth like stars.
I tell the Sybil: "A marvel, truly!
You've told me all my sorrows flawlessly."
Two of Balzac's heroes, amphibian,
Passing behind me as my hand was read,
Told me: "In your own bed you wouldn't dare!"

Fête

Ô gérant du Rat Mort par l'œuf dur engraissé!
   Les fioles de Sherry Brandy qu'on n'a jamais pu déboucher
le dvorak, les menthes, les byrrh
qu'on ne voulut pas déloger de leurs buires
te font, ô gérant, réfléchir.
Sur votre vaste dos, chauffeurs que l'ennui ronge
Sur maints chapeaux fleuris de dames alcooliques
le grand paysage vert du billard se prolonge.
Au dehors, l'auto rit à mourir de colique
Le cadre du damier figure un cimetière
dont les vingt-sept dominos seraient l'ossuaire
et les marbres des tables
sont des grèves de sables.
Ah! que l'aurore, buveurs lyriques,
et tziganes coquets, vous rend mélancoliques!
Or, vous chantez, moineaux de la place Pigalle
chantez l'aurore, l'aurore pâle
et vous aussi sur les chapeaux en vert de gris
Chantez aussi, chantez, poussins aux yeux de verre
Poussins d'oiseaux de Paradis
Cui-cui!
Voulez-vous bien vous taire!

Gala

O Dead Rat manager by boiled eggs enriched!
The flasks of Sherry Brandy they never could uncork
the dvorak, the mint drinks, the Byrrh[186]
they never wanted taken from their crock
make you, o manager, take stock.
On your vast back, chauffeurs' boredom gnaws,
on many flowered hats of lady soaks,
the great green snooker landscape carries on.
Outside, the car will laugh until it croaks,
the checkerboard is like a cemetery
where the checkers are the ossuary
and the tables' marble
are the sandy strands.
Ah! how the dawn, you drinkers lyrical,
and dapper gypsies, makes you melancholical!
Now, you sing, sparrows of Pigalle Plaza,[187]
sing the dawn, the pale dawn,
and you too upon the verdigris hats
sing too, sing, chicks with eyes of glass
chicks of birds of Paradise
Twee-tweet!
Won't you kindly be quiet!

Les purs artistes achètent des autos ▬▬▬

CHRISTOPHE Colomb, c'est Vespuce qui prit ta gloire au
ponant
Gloire d'avoir fait mille esclaves
Qu'on vendit aux Catalans
Approuvé par le conclave
Mais non par le firmament.

Las Casas, auteur sévère
Affirme péremptoirement
Que Colomb sur ses galères
Ne rêvait qu'or et qu'argent
Et ceci le désespère.
Nous en jugeons autrement.

Ah! que nous nous régalions
Au port de ces galions.

Les navires emportaient tous les soleils couchants
Et Colomb s'en allait rechercher dans les Indes
Les cailloux qui portaient le soleil dans leurs flancs.
Il dédiait ses trésors à Marie Rosalinde
Et vouait sa fortune aux églises de marbre.
Les étoiles piquaient déjà les branches d'arbre.
Cabral depuis longtemps abordait au Brésil
Et Colomb de Cuba ne pouvait doubler l'île.
Deux milliers de perdrix ont suivi le bateau.
Empereur, prends-en deux et laisse aller les autres.
Les perdrix se posaient sur les arbres le soir,

Pure Artists Buy Automobiles

CHRISTOPHER Columbus, Vespucci took your glory in
   westerly lands[188]
The glory of many a slave
That were sold to the Catalans
With approval from the conclave
But quite against celestial plans.

Las Casas, no jolly champion[189]
Asserts quite peremptorily
That Columbus in his galleon
Dreamed only monetarily
Which sadly makes him carry on.
And yet we judge quite differently.

Ah! we so gaily feast at rallies
In the harbors of these galleys.

Away the ships brought all the setting suns
Columbus went to feel the Indies' wind
And seek the stones that carry golden suns.
He gave his gold to Mary Rosalind
And his fortune to the marble churches.
Already stars would sting the tree branches.
And Cabral, he had long since found Brazil[190]
While Columbus couldn't pass by Cuba still.
Two thousand partridges followed the boat.
My king, take two and let the others go.
The birds alighted on the trees at dusk,

Et s'éveillaient avec le voyageur transi.

J'ai mes perdrix aussi, ce sont les âmes mortes

Qui colorent mon âme en vert, en jaune, en gris

Qui me disent s'il faut que j'entre ou que je sorte

Que je prenne l'épée, que je tende la main.

Que je serve l'amour ou l'art en mon chemin

J'ai mes trésors aussi qui sont en Amérique

Et qu'aveugle insensé je m'en vais poursuivant

Fier de ma solitude, explorateur aimant.

Awoke with the wayfarer numb with cold.
I too have partridges, all the dead souls
Who color my soul in green, gray, and gold
Who tell me whether to leave or to stay,
To take up the sword, to reach out a hand.
Whether I serve love or art on my way
I too have treasures in America
Which in blindness I pursue with furor
Alone and proud, a loving explorer.

POUR HUIT HEURES DU MATIN

L A lettre n'avait pas le cachet du bureau
De poste et sans l'intérieur on n'aurait su
si venait de Sirius ou bien de Landerneau,
de Pamiers, de Vervins, de Nogent sur la Vire
ce pli mystérieux qu'on hésite à ouvrir
et qui ne fut d'ailleurs qu'un simple prospectus.

POUR NEUF HEURES

Messe! oraison! prière
Songeons à notre heure dernière!
En vérité je te le dis
tu n'iras pas au Paradis
Mais bien plutôt dans les Enfers
si ta poitrine reste en fer,
si tu songes à la poésie
au lieu de suivre pieusement
l'hommage que l'on sert au Très Saint Sacrement.

POUR DIX HEURES

Lettre! ô madame, je n'irai pas
à ces délices, ces repas
que m'offre votre honorée du douze
courant
Solitude ô pénitence douce.

FOR EIGHT O'CLOCK IN THE MORNING

THE letter's provenance, since it had no
   Postmark, unopened would remain obscure:
might come from Sirius or Landerneau,
from Pamiers, or from Vervins or Pont-Aven[191]
this envelope we hesitate to open
and which to boot was but a mere brochure.

FOR NINE O'CLOCK

   Mass! prayer! orison!
   Your final hour think upon!
   Verily I say unto you
   That Paradise is not your path
   Instead you'll suffer all Hell's wrath
   if you remain unrepentant
   and if you think on poetry
   but do not follow piously
   the homage served as Holy Sacrament.

FOR TEN O'CLOCK

   Letter! oh Madame, I do not feel
   I shall go to your delicious meal
   offered by your grace for the tenth
   of this month
   solitude oh sweet penitence.

Madame, loin des falbalas
(Excusez) me voici courant.

POUR ONZE HEURES

Par-delà boulevards fuyons
Fuyons jusques en Castalie
j'emporte tout le Panthéon
dont ma cervelle est nourrie
J'évite un hôte peu chéri.
Par delà boulevards fuyons.

Madame, far from frilly fun
(I beg your pardon) watch me run.

FOR ELEVEN O'CLOCK

To flee beyond the boulevards
To Castalia[192] let us flee
With me I bring the greatest bards
They fill my brain abundantly
This guest I dislike secretly
I flee beyond the boulevards

De quelques invitations

MON confrère Malfilâtre,
Vers divers jeux de loto
Dis-moi pourquoi tu fuis l'âtre
Puisqu'on te guette au ghetto.

Il paraît qu'au téléphone
On n'entend plus que mon nom!
Je voudrais qu'il fût aphone,
S'en servit Agamemnon!

Plaise à celui qu'Antipode
Invite dans ses festins
Dire ce mot « lycopode »
Pour conjurer le destin!

N'étalons, ô mes chaussures,
Nos talents dans les salons!
Je n'ai pas plus de voitures
Que vous n'avez de talons.

Brandis fort au belvédère
Ton instrument opticien!
C'est pour fuir par derrière
Le messager quotidien.

Et si dans une gouttière
Le moineau se trouvait pris,
Agrafez la jarretière
Ce qui signifie mépris.

Concerning Several Invitations

MY dear colleague Malfilâtre[193]
Toward many games of lotto
From home you always scatter
They'll get you in the ghetto.

Seems it is the telephone
They repeat my name upon!
I wish it had no dial tone
Though it were Agamemnon!

Won't you, guest of Antipodes,
Welcome at his revelry
Just say the word "lycopods,"
To dispel that destiny!

O shoes, do not be the stars
Of salons, and do not steal
The show; I have no more cars
Than you, dear shoes, have high heels.

Wave high at the belvedere
Your optic device, very
Practical to steer well clear
Of the day's emissary.

And if into a gutter
A rueful sparrow was borne
You may affix the garter
So it signifies your scorn.

Quoi! le diable est sous la nappe
Et mon cœur est le marteau
Dont il se sert quand il frappe
Pour me séparer de l'eau.

What! The devil is below
My heart, it is the hammer
With which he inflicts the blow
To sever me from water.

Jouer du bugle

Les trois dames qui jouent du bugle
Tard dans leur salle de bains
Ont pour maître un certain mufle
Qui n'est là que le matin.

L'enfant blond qui prend des crabes
Des crabes avec la main
Ne dit pas une syllabe
C'est un fils adultérin.

Trois mères pour cet enfant chauve
Une seule suffisait bien.
Le père est nabab, mais pauvre.
Il le traite comme un chien.

(SIGNATURE)

Cœur des Muses, tu m'aveugles
C'est moi qu'on voit jouer du bugle
Au pont d'Iéna le dimanche
Un écriteau sur la manche.

Playing the Bugle

THREE ladies who play bugle
Late at night in their commodes
Are taught by a dumb yokel
Early on in their abodes.

The blond ephebe who's able
To grab crabs with just one mitt
Pronounces no syllable
He's a bastard, I admit.

Three mothers for this bald son
Where just one he might prefer.
Dad's a nabob, a poor one.
And he treats him like a cur.

(SIGNATURE)

Muse's heart, you blind me well
I'm the one playing bugle
On Jena Bridge[194] on Sunday
Holding a sign on display.

Madame X . . .

Tant bayadères sont tes hanches
Et tes manches,
   Tant peu sages
Tes crabotages de corsage,
   Sur le nu
Ton dentellier tant fendu,
Que si ton chapeau fleuri
   Ne dit oui
Au moins rien jusqu'au chignon
   N'a dit non.

Madame X . . .

So you have such swaying hips
And fingertips,
    Such service
The lattice of your bodice,
    In the nude
All your laced solicitude,
Though your flower hat does not
    Yet say yea,
Nothing, up to your topknot
    Has said nay.

Le bal masqué

L<small>E</small> cristal des buffets en style télégraphique
Se plaint de tes baisers, foule qui le recherche
Glace, lune, les glaces magnifiques
L'abeille des violoncelles y perche
Glace, lune, au foyer de la foule électrique
—Tapis brodé de tigres,—Scapin chanteur, sa trique
Glace, lune, les glaces où luttent
Les grâces des flûtes grasses, les luths.
En ce bal posthume
La foule s'exaspère de n'avoir pas crevé son aposthume
Elle est impertinente. Si peu lui chaut
Le lustre, idéal artichaut
Et qui parle du pôle aux fresques du plafond . . .
. . . Dans le goût de Watteau, des animaux au fond
Et des bateaux légers sur des pins parasols.
(Pins, verdure, à jamais rimeront à Guignol)
Voici Félix et Félicie félicitant la Phénicie
Avec la toque haute la Perse est en velours
Avec la robe longue colorée de vautours.
Les filles d'Actéon et de la Rêverie
Au travers d'Eurotas t'appellent: « Guastalla! »
Et la Grecque Pallas s'installe près d'Allah.
      Aliéné l'habit d'écarlate
      Par un marchand d'occasions
Sosie le sot devient tomate
      Qui fut pâle comme un oignon
      Dame Sosie de mâle rage
      Pleure en pleurs à tel faux balcon

The Masked Ball

CRYSTAL, buffets in telegraphic style
Abhor your kisses, rabble they beguile[195]
Mirror, moon, mirrors unbesmirched
Where bees in violins are perched
Mirror, moon, the heart of the crowd awhile
—Leopard-print carpets—Scapin's[196] song, his smile
Mirror, moon, the mirrors' dispute
Between the graceful glass-blown flutes, the lutes.
Posthumous ball in costume
Where the crowd is inflamed for not having lanced its
      imposthume
And is impertinent. If this mob sneers
At ideal artichokes, the chandeliers
That whisper icy poles to ceiling frescoes . . .
. . . In the manner of Watteau, full of meadows
And airy boats that sail the woodland beauty
(Meadows always rhyme with Punch and Judy)
Felix and Phyllis flatter Phoenicia
With Persia's velvet headgear all in furs
She wears her dress long and streaked with vultures
The daughters Acteon had with Fantasia
Behind Eurotas call on you: "Guastalla!"[197]
And Pallas the Greek sits down close to Allah.
      Of scarlet suit the sale
      Is made by a pawnbroker
Sosie[198] the sap turns red-hot poker
      Who once was onion-pale
      Lady Sosie weeps her tears

On ne sait lequel est moins sage
De la perruque ou du chignon.
Léandre est en soldat, Daphnis en escarbot
L'anxieuse Dorimène en cendrier de verre
Le berger revenu de la montagne claire
Casse des noix sur le parquet de son sabot
Tu brouillais, Aristarque, le tric-trac des quadrilles
Par ton maillot ridé quadrillé d'espadrilles.
Masséna! Masséna! le tailleur de Louis Quinze
Coppélia! Coppélia! danseuse de province.

      « Je crois que ça prend
      Ça me surprend!
      La mésaventure est rare
      Je vous offre un peu de caviar
      Ça se mange avec un cure-dent! »

Les danseurs enseignaient à la foule apostume
L'amour de la géographie par le costume
Les pires venus des Pyrénées,
D'Épire! les minarets de Bénarès
Les chapeaux et les braies du pays calabrais
Et les manches pareilles à des chevaux cabrés
Casques à repasser, vainqueurs à Salamine
Les masques d'un seul nez et de mauvaise mine.

Of rage while in full fig
Which the greater fool appears
The mullet or the wig?
Leander's a bug and Daphnis a recruit[199]
And Dorimène's an ashtray made of glass[200]
The shepherd from the sunny mountain pass
On hardwood breaks the walnuts with his boot
Aristarch, you have a scheme that wrecks[201]
Their czardas; it's your sneaker-checkered spandex.[202]
There's Masséna! Louis XV's tailor[203]
And Coppélia! she's a country dancer.[204]
    "I think it's working
    How surprising!
    It's a rare importunity
    You must try the caviar, really
    Just dip your toothpick in it, darling!"
The dancers taught the crowd a hot abscess[205]
To love geography in native dress
The worst are from the Pyrenees,
Epirus! The minarets of Benares[206]
Calabria and its hats and breeches[207]
Whose sleeves stand up like rearing ponies
Steam iron helms, victors at Salamis[208]
Masks with one nose only, looking nauseous.

Personnages du bal masqué ━━━━━━━━━

HAUTE VIEILLE A L'AIGLE

ROSÉE brillant sur toile d'araignée.
Larme de joie de ta face baignée
    Haute vieille à l'aigle
Corniche à mousse en l'air du monument
Ainsi la lèvre est sur les neuves dents
    Haute vieille à l'aigle.

Characters at the Masked Ball ▰▰▰▰

LOFTY HAG WITH EAGLE

A cobweb's droplets beams of light suffuse.
A joyful tear your misty face bedews
    Lofty hag with eagle
Monument whose mossy cornice hangs
Thus lies the lip upon the tender fangs
    Lofty hag with eagle

Personnages du bal masqué ▄▄▄▄▄▄▄▄▄▄

MARSUPIAUX

Un peu de camomille,
  Lui dit sa fille,
Ou du tilleul?
Lui dit l'aïeul.
—Chéries! vous m'obsédez! non! non!
Pas de coton!
Suis-je une femme ou un garçon?
    Depuis que Matamore
    Est mort
    C'est Marsupiau
    Qu'est dans sa piau.
Jamais de pellicule à ses cheveux bouclés
Le couteau à papier lui servirait de clef
Pour percer tes dossiers, procès du genre humain
Les yeux ont prévenu le travail de la main.
Il n'a jamais pâmé, ni penché, ni péché.
Des goûts exquis, pas de fatigue
Il marche comme une sarigue
On lui voudrait la lance comme au chasseur
La lance? lorsqu'il conduit le bébé de sa sœur?

Honneurs, argent (pas trop) places qu'un autre envie
Bien qu'il dît autrefois: « Moi! Jamais de la vie! »
Il a tout sauf ce qu'il cherche en vain: le danger!
Je ne l'ai jamais vu ni boire ni manger.
Précis dans ses propos, terrible ou plaisantant,

Characters at the Masked Ball ▬▬▬▬

A bit of chamomile?
His daughter smiles
An herbal tea?
Was granny's plea.
"Darlings, don't pester me! No, no!
Please don't coddle!
Am I a molly or a manly model?"
        Since Matamore's[209]
        No more
        It's Marsupio
        Who runs the show.
His curly hair is always dandruff-free
The letter-opener gives him the key
To penetrate your dossier, human race
The eye precedes the hand to judge this case.
He's never slackened, stumbled, slipped or sinned.
Exquisite taste, his health is awesome
He walks like an opossum
In hunter's garb he's not to be sneezed at
A spear? while he leads his sister's brat?

Honor, wealth (just enough), a charming wife
Although he used to say: "Not on your life!"
He has it all, but yearns in vain for danger!
To food and drink he seems a total stranger.
Precise in word, wrathful or good humored,

Cet ange de la guerre est pasteur protestant,
    Depuis que Matamore
    Est mort
    C'est Marsupiau
    Qu'est dans sa piau.

This angel of war is a Lutheran pastor,
    Since Matamore's
    No more
    It's Marsupio
    Who runs the show.

Autres personnages du bal masqué ▬▬▬

J'AI le dos rond, barbe frisant les guêtres
  Point de fessier, voilà ton amoureux
Ululant sous les virgiles résédas de tes fenêtres
Demoiselle de l'entresol aux gants de filet bleu.
Chez toi quand l'horloge sonne
Il en sort un roi sur un rouet
Il a cinq pointes à sa couronne
C'est ton blason, j'en suis blasé
L'ombre du corail bleu ou la pâle améthyste
Les cils d'une fougère
Séparaient la vitre indécise
De la lumière
La fenêtre: un cigare au coin de l'univers.

Craque le silence ou dort sa beauté
Chandelle fidèle d'infidélité
Certaine espérance m'y parle en secret
Les gens de Pampelune
Cherchent dans la lune
Moi je mets un bécarre près de mon cœur
C'est la ligne de flottaison
De la mare et des étoiles
À la maison
Tes souliers t'auraient fait moins mal
La porte intérieure du monde
Est une obscénité

More Characters at the Masked Ball

SERENADE

I'M round-shouldered, my whiskers touch my spats
Without a backside, here's your paramour
Warbling at your window's virgil mignonettes[210]
Damsel of the entresol in gloves of blue velour.
Whenever your clock strikes
Out comes a king on a spinning wheel
Behold his crown's quintuple spikes
And that's your coat of arms, big deal
Blue coral shadows or pale amethyst
The fern's eyelashes
Separate the glass from flashes
Of the light
Window: cigar that dangles from the cosmic lip.

Shatter the silence of her beauty sleep
O candle's faithful infidelity
It nourishes a hope in secrecy
The people of Pamplona[211]
Wish upon the moon-a
But my heart's key signature is natural
And that's what keeps afloat
The lakes and stars alike
At home
Your shoes would have been less painful
The inner gate into the world
Is an obscenity

Je suis comme un cheval qui tremble
De la bride à la peau
Parce que l'amazone porte un oursin.

I am like a horse that trembles
From bridle to pelt
Because the Amazon wears a sea urchin.

Autres personnages du bal masqué ▬▬▬

EN FAMILLE

Nous ne sommes plus de petites filles
Il faut bien apprendre à faire les chapeaux
Et toi-même, frère? . . . Ah! le décepteur!
Laissez-moi, ma mère! il faut le lui dire.
Je lèverai l'œil en haut de la table.
N'as-tu pas cinq doigts comme nous tes sœurs?
N'as-tu pas cinq membres en comptant la tête?
N'as-tu pas cinq sens, la vue et le goût,
L'odorat, l'ouïe? La mère essayait . . .
En haut de la table où ils étaient quatre
La mère en rêvant regardait ses bagues.

Que la table est grande! c'est le Jour des Morts
La salle est brillante, le jour n'est pas blanc
Une étoile est sur votre frère aîné.

More Characters at the Masked Ball ━━━

WE are no longer little girls
   One has to learn how hats are made
And you, brother? . . . Ah! deceiver!
Mother, hush! He needs a lesson.
I'll peek one eye up the table.
Don't you have five fingers like your sisters?
Don't you have five limbs, with your head?
Don't you have five senses, vision,
Taste, smell, hearing? Mother tries to . . .
The four of them looked up the table
At Mother studying her rings.

What a large table! All Soul's Day
The room shines, this is no white day
A star shines upon your brother.

Personnages du bal masqué ▃▃▃▃▃▃▃

MALVINA

V OILÀ qui j'espère vous effraie
    Mademoiselle Malvina ne quitte plus son éventail
Depuis qu'elle est morte.
Son gant gris perle est étoilé d'or.
Elle se tirebouchonne comme une valse tzigane
Elle vient mourir d'amour à ta porte
Près du grès où l'on met les cannes.
Disons qu'elle est morte du diabète
Morte du gros parfum qui lui penchait le cou.
Oh! l'honnête animal! si chaste et si peu fou!
Moins gourmet que gourmande elle était de sang-lourd
Agrégée ès lettres et chargée de cours
C'était en chapeau haut qu'on lui faisait la cour
Or, on ne l'aurait eue qu'à la méthode hussarde
Malvina, ô fantôme, que Dieu te garde!

Characters at the Masked Ball

MALVINA[213]

THIS one I should hope will frighten you
Miss Malvina's never seen without her fan
Since the day she died.
Studded with gold is her pearl-gray glove.
She can twist herself in knots like a gypsy waltz
At your door she dies of love, just beside
The canes along the sandstone walls.
Let's just say she died of diabetes
Killed by the thick perfume that bowed her head
An honest thing, so chaste and undemented!
Less a gourmet than a glutton, moody
She graduated magna cum laude
In top hats they came to court the lady
They'd need an army to seduce the maid
Malvina! God be with you, restless shade.

Autres personnages du bal masqué

Tumulte de chevaux, guerre du mikado
Églantine sur fond d'or
C'est peut-être un cadeau
De mon dernier amant
Il se pend à mon bras
Il m'aime étonnamment
Viol, viole, violon, je suis l'ultra-violet
Je pars pour Chicago
Je me meurs en voiture.

More Characters at the Masked Ball

THUNDER of horses, warrior mikado[214]
Dog-rose[215] against gold leaf
Maybe it's a fond hello
Sent by my latest beau
He hangs on my arm
He loves me stunningly
Vile violin, I'm ultraviolet
I leave for Chicago
I die on the way there.

Autres personnages du bal masqué ▬▬▬

LA DAME AVEUGLE

LA dame aveugle dont les yeux saignent choisit ses mots
Elle ne parle à personne de ses maux

Elle a des cheveux pareils à la mousse
Elle porte des bijoux et des pierreries rousses.

La dame grasse et aveugle dont les yeux saignent
Écrit des lettres polies avec marges et interlignes

Elle prend garde aux plis de sa robe de peluche
Et s'efforce de faire quelque chose de plus

Et si je ne mentionne pas son beau-frère
C'est qu'ici ce jeune homme n'est pas en honneur

Car il s'enivre et fait s'enivrer l'aveugle
Qui rit, qui rit alors et beugle.

More Characters at the Masked Ball ━━━

THE blind lady with the bleeding eyes never wags her tongue
Her dark afflictions all remain unsung

Her mossy hair looks overgrown
She's decked with jewelry and a red gemstone

The blind and portly lady whose eyes are bleeding
Writes nice letters, double-spaced with a generous margin

She's mindful not to wrinkle her plush dress
And struggles for a little more success

And if I don't mention her stepbrother
Well that young man is not so welcome here

Since when he tipples she'll have just a drop
And soon begins to cackle and to yawp.

Autres personnages du bal masqué

RÉPARATEUR perclus de vieux automobiles
L'anachorète hélas a regagné son nid
Par ma barbe je suis trop vieillard pour Paris
L'angle de tes maisons m'entre dans les chevilles
Mon gilet quadrillé a, dit-on, l'air étrusque
Et mon chapeau marron va mal avec mes frusques
Avis! c'est un placard qu'on a mis sur ma porte
Dans ce logis tout sent la peau de chèvre morte.

More Characters at the Masked Ball

OLD crippled automobile repairman
The anchorite's retreated to his hospice
By my beard I'm too old a man for Paris
Your pointy houses jab me in the cnemis[217]
They say my tartan duds appear Etruscan
while my brown hat doesn't match my jerkin
Caution! my threshold placard testified
Inside this hovel smells of dead goat's hide.

DERNIÈRE PARTIE

LAST PART

Arc-en-ciel

C'ÉTAIT l'heure où la nuit fait gémir les montagnes
Les rochers noirs craquaient du pas des animaux,
Les oiseaux s'envolaient des sinistres campagnes
Pour approcher la mer, un meilleur horizon.
Le diable poursuivait un poète en ce temps.
Le poète fixait la mer comme une mort
Car la mer en ce lieu poudrait le cap d'une anse
Et la mer écaillait la peau des rocs immenses.
Mais Jésus, rayonnant de feu derrière la tête,
Portant la croix, vint à monter des rochers noirs.
Le poète a tendu les bras vers le Sauveur
Alors tout s'effaça: la nuit sombre et les bêtes.
Le poète a suivi le Dieu pour son bonheur.

Rainbow

IT was the time when mountains groaned with night
Beneath beast tracks the black boulders would crack,
From sinister lands the birds would take flight
Approaching the sea, a better horizon.
In those days the devil chased a poet.
The poet gazed as if it were death
On the sea foaming the cape of a bay
And chipping skins of the huge rocks away.
But Jesus, haloed with fiery rays,
Carrying the cross, would climb the black rocks.
The poet reached out toward his Savior
And all was erased, the darkness and beasts.
The poet followed the God for his bliss.

Ciel et Terre

Je vois l'amour dans le regard des anges
Je vois le ciel dans le regard de Dieu.
Sans coloris seulement en nuances.
Sans gestes nets des gestes dans les yeux.
Je vois au ciel plus de lentes tendresses
     Que de splendeurs.
Moins de clairons, de joie et de liesses
     Que de douceurs.
Non! je ne veux point d'or, point de couronne
     Au front divin
Point de manteau dont la richesse étonne
     De sceptre en main.
J'entends l'amour dans le bruit des musiques.
L'amour unit le chœur des chers élus.
L'air amoureux par un effet magique
Soutient des saints le cortège confus
Le Corps Sacré du Seigneur Notre Père
Est très mignon, mais fort et bien portant.
Il pense à tous, les morts et les vivants
Aucun souci pourtant sur ce visage
Plus éclairé qu'une aurore au printemps.
Or, pendant que j'écris en ces jours de novembre
Chacun vit enfermé dans sa laideur et dans sa chambre
Sous la voûte des murs que perce le soleil
Dans sa bêtise et sa laideur et dans sa dureté.
La mort a visité l'hôpital du faubourg
Sous les traits d'un vieillard qui désigne les lits.
Le pauvre est sans espoir et le riche a l'ennui

Heaven and Earth

I see love in the gaze of angels
I see the heavens in God's gaze.
Not bright, but in subtle shades.
Gestures not clear, but in the eyes.
In the sky more a slow caress
    Than splendor.
Less fanfare and joy to excess
    But tender.
No! I want no such gold or crown
    On brow divine
No mantle rich to show around
    Nor scepter fine.
I hear love in the sound of music.
Love unites the chosen choir
The loving air's effect is magic
It sustains the saints' muddled march
The Sacred Body of Our Father
Has charm, but is robust and strong.
He thinks of those alive or dead
His face is tranquil all along
And lit up like the dawn in spring.
Now as I write this in November days
As all are locked in rooms and in malaise
Beneath the arch of walls pierced through with sun
In hard-heartedness, stupidity and ugliness.
Death stops by at the faubourg hospital
As an old man who points out certain beds.
The poor despair, ennui torments the rich

Le marin sans secours, le soldat sans abri.
La joie cache la haine et la haine l'envie.
Voici l'affolement et l'horrible plaisir
Voici le désespoir, l'alcool et le désir!
Et le vrombissement des machines de fer
Semble le cri d'un monde qui ressemble à l'enfer.
Le Seigneur aux humains signifie sa lumière
Chacun de nous du ciel a l'image en son cœur.
Il peut le conquérir avant l'heure dernière.
Et trouver en son Dieu la Paix et le bonheur.
Espérons! espérons en sa miséricorde
À qui sait demander le Seigneur dit: « J'accorde! »
Le Seigneur à la fois donne épreuve et salut
Il nous fait concevoir le bonheur des élus
Pour qu'à le mériter nous mettions plus de zèle
Aimons-nous! Aimons Dieu! Et l'amour a des ailes.

None help the sailor, nor shelter the soldier.
Joy hides the hatred, the hatred hides envy.
Here there is terror and horrible pleasures
Here there is hopelessness, liquor, and hungers!
The drone of steel machines will groan and swell
And the world's cry is of a place like hell.
The Lord to people signifies his light
In every heart is graven heaven's image
One may conquer it before the night
Goodness and Peace in God one may envisage.
Let us hope! Let us hope in all his mercy
To one who asks, the Lord says, "It is granted."
The Lord gives both the trial and salvation
Thus we must guess the rapture of the chosen
So that we strive for it with all our might
Let us love! Let us love God! Love takes flight.

Renaissance de l'esprit religieux

C'EST pas boulonné comme un pont en fer, les églises.
Il faut la permission de Jésus-Christ pour que ça se
     détruise.
    C'est un objet en améthyste
    Et en saphir bleu
    Dont l'entrepreneur en bâtisse
    Est le fils de Dieu.
C'est gardé par certains anges policiers très fins
On dirait des candélabres, c'est des séraphins.
Quels agrès parent leur cher jeu?
Qui donc équipa leurs cierges?

    Ça repose sur des choses roses
    Qui n'ont l'air de rien,
    Et tu ne peux, même si tu l'oses,
    Y mettre la main.

Des plans du futur les patriarches sont mandataires
Ils y passeront toute l'éternité, Dieu les regarde faire.
N'aie donc pas peur, pauvre terre,
On travaille pour toi.
Il y a des génies planétaires
Au-dessus des toits.
L'Église est penchée sur la terre
Pour nous soulager dans nos guerres;
Elle est suivie par les infirmières,
Les paysans et les débonnaires.

Rebirth of Religious Spirit

CHURCHES, they ain't bolted together like a steel bridge.
It takes Jesus' permission to destroy 'em.
    It's made of sapphire or
    Of amethyst: the one
    Who's the building contractor
    Is God's only true son.
It's guarded by some angels, they're quite slim
They look like candelabra, but they're seraphim.
What tackle graces all their darling capers?
And who lit up their noble tapers?

It rests on many a pink thingy
With an insubstantial air,
And you can't, not even if you dare,
Upon them lay a pinky.

For future plans the patriarchs are delegated
And for all time God sees them do what he's dictated.
So, poor earth, don't you be afraid
For you there's work non-stop.
There are planetary geniuses arrayed
Over every rooftop.
The Church is leaning over all the land
Providing solace when a war's at hand;
Behind the Church the nurse will follow,
The peasant, the good-natured fellow.

Déjà, bien avant Jésus-Christ,
Les oracles perdaient leur crédit.
Diagoras et Cicéron,
Xénophane de Colophon
Récusent
Les ventres des poulets où jouent les Élohim.
Votre livre des Papes, calabrais Joachim
Et tes lyriques centuries Nostradamus
Les sages s'en moquaient, la science les dénonce.
Le grand Art des Toscans revient avec le nonce.
Jubilé! jubilé de la nubilité.
Mon enfant, montre-nous ta sopranilité.
L'Ararat monopolise les cris de l'Électricité.

Le pavé de la Capitale
Est tout lavé d'apparitions.
Au « filet de sole » une étoile
Fit lâcher un plat de poissons.
Campagne, ô ma verte promise.
Bois de Boulogne, nouvelle église,
Qui de mes vers sera l'éternelle fiancée
Près du lac, œil si contrefait
Que Phébus recule à le voir
Et préfère les Ninivites qui s'obsèdent sur les trottoirs;
Sur un arbre en forme de croix,
Un garde a vu Jésus lui-même,
Et, prêt à mourir pour la Foi,
C'est à Charenton qu'on le mène.
Un ange vient qui le délivre.

Already, well before Jesus Christ,
The oracles were losing credit
Diagoras and Cicero
Xenophanes of Colophon[218]
Jettison
The chicken's stomachs in which frolic Elohim.
With your book of Popes, Calabrian Joachim
And your lyric centuries, o Nostradamus[219]
The wise once scoffed at what our science spurns.
with the nuncio the Tuscan's great Art returns.
Jubilee! jubilee of nubility.
My child, show us all your sopranility.
Ararat[220] monopolizes cries of Electricity.

The paving of the Capital
Is quite washed of apparitions.
With "sole filets" a star let fall
A plateful of fish from the oceans.
Bois de Boulogne, my green bride,[221]
And the new church of countryside,
To whom my verse shall be eternally engaged
Near the lake, an eye so distorted
That Phoebus retreats at its sight,
And prefers the Ninivites hounding each other on sidewalks;
On a tree shaped just like a cross,
A guard has seen Jesus himself,
And ready to die for the Faith,
Off to Charenton[222] he's taken.
An angel soon delivers him.

Au Bon Marché, grand magasin,
—Tout s'y vend, excepté mes livres—
Les gens venus là pour rien.
Ceux qui sont venus pour emplettes,
Sans qu'on les en pût empêcher,
Sont à genoux devant l'apparition céleste.
Ils reçoivent la rémission de leurs péchés.

Une dame a vu Dieu pendant qu'elle était au bain,
Elle a sonné pour qu'on aille chercher le médecin.
Ortiz de Zarate, qui est un bon peintre,
A vu Dieu comme un triangle dans un cintre,
L'imagier-poète nommé Georges Delaw
A vu Dieu au ventre avec une barbe slave.

Et moi qui suis plus bête que le gardien du bois,
Je vous jure, ô mon Dieu, d'observer vos lois,
Car j'ai vu votre Auguste Face et votre robe.
Au devoir de le déclarer que jamais je ne me dérobe!
Et toi qui sens mes larmes au travers de ces lignes,
Songe que de la Vérité elles sont les signes.
Démon! démon! que tu me navres.

Sachez! l'Amalécite est mort,
Nous avons veillé son cadavre,
Tout fiers d'avoir atteint le port.

At Bon Marché, department store,
—It's all for sale, but not my books—
The people have come, but what for?
Those who have come to buy some things,
It proves impossible to keep them
From kneeling before the divine apparition.
They receive the remission of their sins.

As she bathed a lady saw God; she rang her
Servants to send for the doctor.
Ortiz de Zárate, who is a good painter,[223]
Saw God as a triangle in a clothes hanger,
The poet in images named Georges Delaw[224]
Saw God with a belly and Slavic whiskers.

And I, dumber than the park-keeper
I swear, o God, to keep your laws:
I saw your robes, your August Countenance.
It is a duty to declare it, and never countenance
Shirking! You who sense my tears through these lines,
Recall they are of Truth the signs.
Demon! demon! how you dismay me.

Know this! the Amalekite's dead,[225]
For we sat with his dead body,
So proud to see our port ahead.

Micomusa, l'ornithologue
Et l'éphèbe paillard et gourmand
Qui nous disait des monologues
Furent bénis aux Quatre-Temps.
À l'aube, hier, quai de Grenelle,
Un cheval et son cavalier
Se sont cabrés, droits sur la selle,
Voyant au ciel un bouclier.

Président de la République,
Quel beau titre as-tu hérité!
L'auto de vérité s'oblique,
Hérites-tu la vérité?

Et toi, l'enfer des mille bêtes,
Sénat, Chambre des députés,
Quand donc—tel on voit les huissiers,
L'ange ira-t-il de tête en tête,
Mais pour les faire communier.
Promeneurs, meneurs solitaires
Tournant autour de vos tourments,
La vérité est sur la terre,
Vous pouvez enlever vos gants.

Micomusa, the ornithologist[226]
And that ephebe, rapacious and bawdy,
Of whose monologues we got the gist,
Were blessed at the Quatre-Temps.[227]
At dawn the other day, quai de Grenelle,[228]
A horse and his rider reared up
And stood straight up in the saddle,
Seeing a shield in the heavens, high up.

President of this Republic,
You've come into such a lovely title!
The car of truth may veer oblique,
To the truth are you entitled?

And you, hell of a thousand beasts,
Senate, Chamber of Deputies,
When will the angel like a repo man
Pass from head to head: to give communion.
Those who stroll, lonely ringleaders
Circling your every torment,
The truth is found right here on earth,
So you may now remove your gloves.

ENVOI

Napoléon et Talleyrand,
Je vous prie, descendez d'un cran,
Jésus l'a dit: « Le premier rang
Est réservé aux bons enfants. »

NOTA-BENE

Le retour en France des robes de bure
Aurait figuré dans ces écritures,
Mais ce qui réalise la poésie de Dieu,
Vouloir l'expliquer, c'est vouloir faire mieux.

ENVOY

Napoleon and Talleyrand,[229]
I pray you, you must stand
further down; you must understand
What Jesus said: children command.

NOTA BENE

The French return to the old monk's habit
Might well have figured in the present writ,
Yet this poetry of God, its strictest letter
To explain it is to want to do better.

Comme Marie-Madeleine

Mon Dieu, vous m'avez fait une âme solitaire
Vous m'avez mis au cœur des zones militaires
Ces fortifs désertés par les propriétaires.
Mon Dieu, vous m'avez fait une âme monastique
Une âme désolée d'être privée de vous
Aspirant à l'astral, soucieuse d'esthétique
Centrifuge comme l'épine sur la feuille du houx
Et vous m'aviez aussi gréé pour les tendresses
Des échelles écoutez les longs gémissements
C'est le vent de l'amour, Seigneur, dans mes haubans
L'amour, mon Dieu! dites l'orage et la détresse

> Cœur bien éperonné
> Luminaire de l'idéalité
> Alors, quelle fêlure?
> Hélas! la luxure!

Like Mary Magdalene

My God, you've made my soul solitary
You've placed in my heart these military
Zones, strongholds deserted by their owners.
My God, you've made my soul monastic
A soul sorry to be deprived of you
Reaching for stars, thinking the esthetic
Centrifugal as thorns on holly leaves
And you had rigged me too for tenderness
Hear how the ladders groan and groan out loud
It's the wind of love, Lord, caught in my shrouds
Love, my God! call it tempest and distress

> My heart is spurred along
> The ideal luminaire shines on
> What flaw, then?
> Alas! in lust and passion!

Le pêcheur et l'autre

CE n'est pas moi qui vis
Ce n'est pas moi qui prie
Il y a un moine au pied de l'autel
Il y a un moine à la grille, à la grille de l'autel
Là-bas est une ville dans la brume
Entre les arbres et les feuillages des arbres
Il y a le ciel, il y a les toits qui fument
Et trois clochers qui piquent.
« Tu as bien tort, mon ami, de vivre de l'argent d'une femme
—Oh! qu'on est bien dans son fauteuil
—Et moi j'ai tort de t'en parler
Car j'ai un amour inavouable dans le cœur. »
Ce n'est pas moi qui vis
Ce n'est pas moi qui prie
Il y a un moine à la grille, à la grille de l'autel.
Moi, j'ai un amour inavouable
Là-bas est une ville dans la brume
Les donjons d'usine et les tours et les clochers d'une ville.
Si la paix est dans la ville
Elle n'est pas dans mon cœur.
Tu as bien tort, mon ami, d'accepter les cigares de la dame.
Mais moi j'ai un amour, un amour inavouable dans le cœur.

The Sinner and the Other

Iᴛ's not me who lives
It's not me who prays
There's a monk at the foot of the altar
There's a monk at the screen, the screen of the altar
Far off is a city in the mist
Between the trees and their foliage
There is the sky, there are the smoking roofs
And three steeples poking up.
"You are quite wrong, my friend, to live on a woman's money"
"Oh! I'm quite comfy in my chair"
"And I'm wrong to speak to you about it
For I've got a shameful love in my heart."
It's not me who lives
It's not me who prays
There's a monk at the screen, the screen of the altar.
For my part I've got a shameful love
Far off is a city in the mist
The factory strongholds and a city's towers and steeples.
If there's peace in the city
There's none in my heart.
You're quite wrong, my friend, to accept the lady's cigars.
But me, I've got a love, a shameful love in my heart.

Méditation pour le jour de Noël

ESPRIT descendu dans la grotte
Comme l'inspiration sur le front du génie
Illuminez le cœur des hommes.
Plus de serpent et plus de bêtise
L'intelligence est un dépôt
Que Jésus laissa dans la terre
Et tous les génies qu'on révère
Valent par le Grand Génie d'en haut.
Embellissez de fleurs la face des écoles
Éclairez en festons les sièges enseignants.
Exultons et chantons, faisons des farandoles.
C'est aujourd'hui Noël la fête des savants
Naissance de l'Esprit, ô saint anniversaire
Je t'appelle, Noël, la fête des Lumières
Gardez! Gardons l'humilité: de l'esprit c'est l'amorce
Dit dans la grotte l'enfant nu
Et gardez, gardons la candeur: de l'esprit, c'est la force.
Dit un berger des peaux de ses moutons vêtu.
Mais le pied de Satan au bord du chou de mes entrailles . . .
Prince stupide mais puissant.
—Adieu, dit l'Esprit Saint, il faut que je m'en aille.
—Hélas! à toutes les horreurs je m'attends.

Meditation for Christmas Day

SPIRIT descended to the grotto
Upon the brow of genius, inspiration
Illuminate the hearts of men.
No more serpent, no more dullness
Intelligence is a deposit
That Jesus left upon the earth
Upon all geniuses revered
The Great Genius above bestowed their worth.
Light teachers' chairs with banners, decorate
With flowers the façades of all the schools.
We'll sing, exult, and dance in farandoles.
On Christmas day, savants shall celebrate
The Spirit's birth, oh holy birthday,
Noel, I call you festival of Lights today
Keep, let us keep humility: it is the spirit's spark
The naked child in the grotto says
And keep, let us keep this candor: the strong spirit's mark.
The shepherd in his sheepskin says.
But Satan's hoof so near the apple of my entrails . . .
A stupid prince, yet powerful.
—Farewell! away the Holy Spirit sails.
—Alas! the horrors I expect are awful.

GASPARD de Coligny en velours sur fond d'or
Priait. Priaient aussi les rois et les corrégidors;
Les marchands, les docteurs, petits et grands artistes
Priaient; les ouvriers, les pèlerins, mères, pères et fils,
Les soldats, les capitaines, les bourgeois priaient.
Saint-Louis de ses forêts faisait des cathédrales
Des voûtes d'un palais celles d'un hôpital
Louis XIV et ses femmes, les courtisans priaient.
Sous Louis XV on niait; nier, c'est toujours croire
Et les abbés poudrés confessaient après boire
Néron narguait les Dieux que craignait Marc-Aurèle
Et l'homme à Dieu toujours construisit des autels.
Pasteur avait Jésus, les Papous ont Moloch.
Mais vous, du cercle noir de votre indifférence!
De votre muet orgueil, ô trop heureuse France!
Tranchez l'Esprit divin de toutes les époques.

Juillet 1920

GASPARD II de Coligny in velours[230]
Prayed. Prayed also kings and corregidors;
Merchants and doctors, artists small and great
Prayed; workers, pilgrims, mothers, fathers, sons,
Soldiers, captains, property owners prayed.
Saint Louis out of forests built cathedrals,[231]
And palace arches, those of hospitals
Louis XIV, his wives, his courtiers prayed.
Under Louis XV, negation's still belief[232]
Their confessions follow sin's aperitif
Nero mocked the Gods Marcus Aurelius feared
And mankind our God has always revered.
Pasteur had Jesus, Papuans, Moloch.[233]
But from the black orb of your indifference,
From your prideful silence, too blessed France!
You cut God's Spirit from every epoch.

July 1920

Verre de sang

à Juan Gris

LES idées autour du Brocken et les cœurs autour du Calvaire.
Les unes sont couleur des temps
Les autres sont couleur du sang
De votre sang j'avais bu la moitié d'un verre
J'ai jeté l'autre sur la mer
Il en naquit un grand vaisseau
Avec un acrobate en vert
Sur le bout du mat grand'arrière
Tous les morts gémissaient sous la forme de vagues
Et les damnés tendaient le dos des rochers noirs
Les plaints des vivants se tordaient dans les algues
Les horribles joyeux, les plus horribles tristes
Dans la cale comme en 93 les prisons
Les fatigues, les chiens savants et les gradés
Les femmes roublardes douloureuses.
Le bruit fatal des vagues est en marge
Et l'humanité sur le bateau jouait aux cartes
Un ministre d'État y lisait son destin
Sur le grand'arrière.
À quoi bon tout le sang versé sur le calvaire
Pour ce bateau montant sur les vagues des morts?
Il faut souffrir puisqu'il faut vivre et qu'il faut voir
La tache du sang rouge atteignit les rochers
Tout frémissait, ma lyre aussi,
Et le vaisseau portait toute l'humanité
Moi je connais une boutique teinte du sang du Seigneur

Glass of Blood

For Juan Gris[234]

I DEAS around the Brocken and hearts around mount
    Calvary[235]
Some are the color of days
Others are a blood red haze
Of your blood I had drunk half a decanter
I threw the other half upon the water
From it was born a great vessel
An acrobat in green aglitter
Upon the end of the mast furthest aft
All of the dead groaned in the form of waves
And the damned stretched out their backs' black rocks
Cries of the living twisted in seaweed
The horrible gleeful, the sad more horrible
In the hold like the prisons in '93[236]
Exhaustions, performing dogs, officers
And wily mournful women.
The fateful sound of waves in the margins
And on the boat humanity played cards
A minister of state read his fortune there
Furthest aft.
Why all the blood spilled at Calvary
For this ship mounting the waves of the dead?
There must be suffering for there must be life and vision
The red bloodstain reached even to the rocks
Everything was quivering, my lyre as well,
And the vessel carried all of humanity

Mais le « successeur » frénétique
Y fait mettre un drapeau de la même couleur
Le ciel est aujourd'hui rouge du sang du Christ
Mais sur moi, terrifié contre un vase de marbre
Dans le Luxembourg plein de fleurs
Le sanglier sorti des arbres
A jeté ses cornes d'or et sa fureur
Demain l'hiver viendra faner les capucines
Et moi je songerai, Seigneur, qu'on t'assassine.
L'air du nord a cicatrisé les plaies.

As for me, I know a boutique tinted with the blood of the Lord
But the frenetic "successor"
Has a flag put there in the same color
The sky today is red with Christ's red blood
Yet upon me, trembling against a marble vase
In the flowery Luxembourg garden
The wild boar that left the trees
Has thrown his golden tusks and his fury
Tomorrow the nasturtiums will have withered
And I will see, Lord, how you are murdered.
The northern air has scarred over the wounds.

Passage de la terre. Épreuve de nos sens.
Donnez-moi! donnez-moi d'en comprendre le sens.
Ami Présent Parfait! Ami si Pur! Ami Présent
La nature et la vie! Ce sont là vos présents
Je les prends et m'applique à en faire bon usage,
C'est-à-dire d'exercer pour devenir plus sage
Ce que j'ai d'esprit, de sentiment et de cœur
Vous êtes à votre fenêtre et Vous pensez à mon bonheur
Moi je cours à ma perte et sans comprendre vos mystères
Vous m'avez fait pour le ciel et je me donne à la terre
Ce que vous m'avez donné pour m'être divinement salutaire
Je m'en sers pour ce qui est le contraire
Et je fais mon mal et celui des autres.
Je suis le vilain séducteur et je devais être un apôtre.
Convertissez-moi! Convertissez-moi! Convertissez-moi!

EARTH's passing. Trial of every sense.
Allow me! allow me to understand its sense.
Perfect Present Friend! Friend so pure! Presence
Nature and life! These are your presents
I take them and try to use them wisely,
In service of wisdom, to do my part
With all my mind, my feeling and my heart
You're at your window and You consider my happiness
But I run to my ruin and fail to understand your mysteries
You made me for the heavens and I give myself to earth
What you've given me as divinely salutary
I use it for that which is contrary
And I do evil to myself and others.
I am the base seducer and I should have been an apostle.
Convert me! Convert me! Convert me!

Un ménage d'artistes sans Dieu

MAGICIEN qui remue les hommes des photos
Et qui sait faire partir les voitures sans chevaux
Pourrais-tu pas aussi donner un coup de lime
Au caractère affreux de mon illégitime?
L'Église le pourrait, le Démon le défend.
Paris, ville magnifique
Où l'arbre n'est pas taillé
Il manque à ta République
Contre lui de batailler
Du dernier des progrès l'empire de Satan dépend.

Les serpents enlacés faisaient mes initiales
Le linge qui séchait derrière l'hôpital
On les lisait encore aux croches des sonates
Les dames les tressaient avec leurs nattes.
Leurs jambages font ton ombre, ô Trocadéro
Et tes poutrelles, balcon vide du Métro
Mais le soir, tous les soirs me ramène au foyer
J'ai ma femme et son chien: j'entends aboyer.

A Godless Artists' Household

WIZARD who makes the folks in photos move
    For whom the carts depart without a horse
And could you perhaps apply the file
To her temperament, which I revile?
What the Church could do, the Devil forbids.
Paris, magnificent town
Whose trees they never cut back
Your republic lets us down
On him they launch no attack
Upon the latest progress Satan counts.

The coiled snakes signed with my initials[237]
Laundry drying in back of hospitals
They reappear in this sonata's quavers
The ladies plaited them into their braids.
Their downstrokes cast your shade, o Trocadero[238]
And your posts, empty Metro balcony
But at night, each night brings me back to hearken
To my wife and her dog: I hear barking.

Méditation sur la mort ━━━━━━━

V OICI la noire mort et toute sa misère
Le but des buts; de l'eau sur de la terre
Des os pourris au cimetière
La chair ne compte plus.
C'est moins utile que de la pierre.
Horreur! toucher cela quand on est bien portant!
Pourtant! trois fleurs . . . trois pleurs!
Paquet, va-t'en! Il y a bien le monument
Épitaphe, discours éloquents.
Qu'importe si ta dernière heure
Ne vous appartient pas, Seigneur
Alors . . . le silence! Quel oubli.

Un locataire a pris ta place
On a vendu l'armoire, l'armoire à glace
Le lit
Ces gens qui passent dans la rue
Parleraient-ils du disparu?
Pleure aujourd'hui sur ta misère
Songe mieux à ton heure dernière.

Deux troupes d'anges et de démons
Se disputent le moribond
Je me connais: je les verrai:
Tout est calme, sauf mes traits
J'assiste à l'Éternel décret.
Les démons! . . . ah! que je m'en tire!
Oh! faites-moi recommencer! Seigneur plutôt le martyre.
Trop tard! Je suis nu devant Dieu.

Meditation on Death

HERE is the blackness of death, its wretchedness
The goal of goals, and water over earth
Rotten bones in the cemetery
Flesh no longer counts.
It's less useful than stone.
The horror! touching this when in good health!
And yet! three flowers . . . three sobs!
Bundle, off with you! There's still the monument
Epitaph, speeches so eloquent.
What does it matter if your final moment
Does not belong to you, good Lord
Then . . . the silence! Such oblivion.

A tenant has taken your place
The wardrobe's been sold, the one with the mirror
The bed
These people passing in the street
Might they be speaking of the deceased?
Weep this day upon your wretchedness
Think further on your final hour.

Two bands of angels and demons
Fight over the dying man
I know myself: I will see them:
All is calm except my face
I face the Eternal decree.
The demons! . . . ah! let me pull through!
Oh! help me start over! Lord, martyrdom instead.
Too late! I am bare before God.

Mémoire d'un méchant démon, rageur et radieux
De ma vie ce fut le témoin
Quant à l'ange il ne parle point.
Bonnes intentions, mais faible et sot
Il se rendait au moindre assaut.
Allons! toi qui t'écris ces lignes
Eh bien quoi il n'est pas trop tard
Au lieu de vivre en lézard
Fuis les influences malignes
Coupe, tranche, épluche ton rôle
Demande à Dieu un coup d'épaule
Tu te reposeras sûrement
La veille de ton enterrement.

Memoirs of a cruel demon, enraged and radiant
Of my life he was the witness
But the angel remains speechless.
Good-intentioned, weak and witless
He gave up before every fight.
Come on! you who writes these verses
Well now the time is not yet past
Quit your lounging like a lizard
And flee malign influences
Cut, slice, and peel your role away
And ask God for the old heave-ho
You'll surely have a proper doze
The eve of your final repose.

Litanies de la Sainte Vierge

Vierge si merveilleusement chatoyante qu'elle reflète les lumières du Saint-Esprit
Vierge si uniquement pareille au ciel que le Ciel l'épousa.
Seule mère possible pour le Seigneur
Enfant de quinze ans qui a parlé à l'Ange
Honorée d'un mariage avec Dieu
Honorée de la maternité de Dieu
Mère et épouse du ciel
Miraculée, miraculeuse
Gardienne du trésor unique
Gardienne du trésor de la terre
Gardienne du trésor du ciel
Mère d'espoir et d'angoisse
Entrailles divinisées
Providence de Dieu, Providence des hommes
Bergère de l'Agneau pascal
Mère qui a vu grandir l'Homme
Mère qui a vu souffrir l'Homme
Mère qui a vu mourir l'Homme
Mère confiante, mère émerveillée
Éternelle impératrice des chrétiens
Impératrice à la cour des Parfaits
Impératrice humble
Impératrice intangible, attentive, sensible, juste, savante et pure
Escalier de la Perfection
Trône de la Perfection
Jardinière de nos âmes
Lampe de nos veilles

Litanies of the Holy Virgin

VIRGIN so marvelously shimmering that she reflects the
light of the Holy Spirit
Virgin so uniquely like the heavens that the Heavens married
her.
Sole mother possible for the Lord
Child of fifteen who spoke to the Angel
Honored by a marriage to God
Honored by becoming mother to God
Mother and Wife of the heavens
Miraculously saved, miraculous herself
Guardian of the unique treasure
Guardian of the treasure of the earth
Guardian of the treasure of the heavens
Mother of hope and anguish
Womb made divine
God's Providence, Providence of men
Shepherdess of the Paschal lamb
Mother who saw Man grow
Mother who saw Man suffer
Mother who saw Man die
Confident mother, mother amazed
Eternal empress of Christians
Empress at the court of the Perfect
Humble empress
Intangible, attentive, sensitive, just, learned and pure empress
Stairwell of Perfection
Throne of Perfection
Gardener of our souls

Présidente de nos assemblées
Infirmière de nos faiblesses
Robe couleur d'aiguille
Toute à chacun, tout pour chacun
Émeraude du ciel
Diamant des nuits
Topaze des jours.
Mère du Verbe, force du génie, muse des arts,
Vie de la pensée, pensée de la vie
Ô jeune fille pour toujours
Ô jeune mère pour toujours
Ô pureté pour toujours
Ô beauté
Sauvez les âmes de mes amis morts à la guerre.

Lamp of our vigils
President of our assemblies
Nurse of our weaknesses
Gown the color of needles
Entirely with each person, for each person
Emerald of the heavens
Diamond of nights
Topaz of days.
Mother of the Word, strength of genius, art's muse,
Life of the mind, mind of life
O young lady forever after
O young mother forever after
O purity forever after
O beauty
Save the souls of my friends who died at war.

TRANSLATOR'S NOTES

1. Georges Auric (1899–1983), distinguished French composer and musician, member of Les Six, a group of composers associated with Erik Satie and Jean Cocteau, also friends of Jacob. After early years as an avant-garde composer with Les Six, Auric wrote music for films, including Cocteau's seminal *Blood of a Poet*.

2. On Max Jacob's early friendship with Picasso, see my introduction, and the exhaustive Hélène Seckel, Emmanuelle Chevrière, Helene Henry, et al., *Max Jacob et Picasso* (Paris: Réunion des Musées Nationaux, 1994). Jacob was indeed present at times with Picasso in Spain, particularly in Barcelona and in Céret, a Catalonian village at the foot of the French Pyrenees where cubism flourished between 1911 and 1913 (some artists returned there after World War I). After these voyages of 1912 and 1913 in Picasso's company, Jacob would visit Madrid and other parts of Spain on his own in 1926.

3. Alicante is a city in the Valencian Community of Spain, and a Mediterranean port.

4. Annuities are an insurance contract providing a revenue stream over a period of time, sometimes for an entire lifetime. This is a rough equivalent to *rentes*, a general term for periodic revenue for which one does not work, associated with the nineteenth-century bourgeoisie in France. Oddly, Jacob would benefit from insurance annuities from 1932 until his death, after a car accident in 1929.

5. The heraldry of Castille traditionally consists of the facade of a yellow castle on a red background.

6. An opéra-comique has spoken parts alternating with songs. The théâtre de l'Opéra-Comique, known as the salle Favart, was founded in 1714, and still stands today as a historical monument. Major operas of this repertoire include *Carmen*, *Manon*, and *Les Filles du regiment*. It remains unclear which opera Jacob has in mind, but see my introduction on Jacob and operatic genres generally.

7. By "Phrygian Catalans," Jacob presumably means people wearing something like Phrygian caps, also known as liberty caps, a soft conical cap with a bent tip.

8. Rascasse or *Scorpaena scrofa*, known as the red scorpionfish, is a venomous fish native to the Eastern Atlantic and the Mediterranean, and is a traditional ingredient in the seafood stew known as bouillabaisse.

9. I have not been able to identify any "Caiman Square" in Spain, and the location may be imaginary.

10. Possibly an allusion to the poetry of *Contes d'Espagne et d'Italie* (1829), the first book of poems published by Alfred de Musset, a second-generation French Romantic poet (he was only nineteen at the time). But Jacob may have any of a number of descriptions in mind by this Romantic poet, who also wrote stories set in Spain.

11. A porte-cochère is a large gate allowing the passage of motorized vehicles or carriages, frequently seen in European architecture.

12. Figueres is a city in Catalonia, eighty-seven miles from Barcelona.

13. The Pathé Brothers was one of the two largest cinema production companies in France, along with Gaumont. Pathé was founded in 1896 and was for many years the largest such company in the world. The two competing film companies, Gaumont and Pathé, finally merged in 2001.

14. *Allioideae* is a plant subfamily including the allium genus (of which onions, shallots, and garlic are examples). Many allioideae have highly decorative star-shaped flowers gathered in a ball at the top of a long stalk.

15. Presumably, Napoleon Bonaparte is the emperor in question; his campaign in Spain lasted from 1807 until his final defeat in 1814. The Spanish did not regard Napoleon as a liberator and resisted his rule throughout the campaign.

16. On these lines, which allude to Mallarmé's poem "The Azure," see the translator's introduction.

17. This line, with a slight variation, recurs in "A Godless Artists' Household."

18. Jacob was deeply familiar with François de Sales's *Introduction to the Devout Life*. In later years, he became a practitioner of daily written meditations, always based on basic Christian themes drawn from François de Sales's book.

19. The last word is *glace*, which can mean "ice," "ice cream," or "mirror"; the meaning of the verse is somewhat obscure, but Jacob suggests that all these minds are to be sacrificed in the name of the war effort (the poem is dated April 1910, well before World War I).

20. Tartana is a Spanish term for a kind of covered carriage.

21. J. P. Morgan, the banker and financier of J. P. Morgan Chase.

22. Epsom is a city in England, once a popular spa town, and origin of the term "Epsom salts" (the waters of Epsom are rich in magnesium sulphate, the other name for this mineral). In the original poem, Jacob instead mentions Collioure, a picturesque Mediterranean village.

23. Jacob uses the extremely rare verb *feuilloler*, meaning "to become covered with leaves" (like a tree in the Spring, for instance); Apollinaire uses the verb several times in *Alcools*, and Jacob's use of the word reads like an echo of Apollinaire.

24. Calixte is a male first name meaning "the most beautiful," associated with the name of the mythological nymph Callisto, which has the same meaning.

25. In Ovid's *Metamorphoses*, Apollo chases Daphne for a kiss, but the latter is transformed into a laurel, which hence becomes a sign of (poetic) honor.

26. *Evoheh* or *evohe* is an ancient Greek expression of Bacchic frenzy or enthusiasm.

27. The quincunx pattern is a common mode for planting trees in orchards and other domestic spaces throughout France.

28. The verb is used intransitively by Jacob.

29. The Odet is the river that runs through Jacob's native city of Quimper.

30. Septimia Zenobia was a glorious third-century Syrian queen known for having attempted to secede from the Roman empire and for her tolerance of religious minorities. She has inspired many tales—hence her mention by Jacob.

31. "Moral death" recurs in Jacob's work and letters as the expression designating what Americans might call being "born again" in a specifically Christian sense. The apocalyptic poem that follows is hence an allegory of the inner turmoil that leads to transformation, and from there to salvation.

32. The Pont-Neuf is Paris's oldest surviving bridge.

33. François-Noël Babeuf, known as Gracchus Babeuf (1760–1797) was a socialist activist of the French Revolution. He proposed the abolition of private property, vehemently opposed the Directory, and defended the poor. Jacob, politically conservative, was anticommunist; Babeuf is a symptom of the general catastrophe in this poem.

34. "Dolmans" seems to be a metonym for soldiers wearing dolmans, here probably referring to the short jacket worn by hussars (Paris is being overrun by foreign soldiers, evidently).

35. Rue Quincampoix is a street near the church of Saint-Merri on the right bank of Paris. There is apparently no historical connection of this street to the Carmelites mentioned here.

36. Cancale is a city on the Northern coast of Brittany known for its oysters.

37. Doctor Claude Benoiste was the director of the Sanatorium de Kerpape, a sanatorium situated in Ploemeur, near Lorient. Jacob stayed there on various occasions and was a good friend of the doctor.

38. Avranches is a small city at the southern edge of Normandy. Its sands are not particularly well-known or unusual, though it is a coastal city.

39. Jean-Henri Latude, sometimes known as Masers de Latude, was a French writer best known for his *Despotisme dévoilé*, a work recounting his thirty-five or so years of imprisonment in the Bastille and other state prisons between 1749 and his death in 1805. In 1749, he had sent a poisoned box to the Marquise de Pompadour, simultaneously warning her of the attempt on her life, in order to curry favor; the trick failed and Pompadour sent him to prison, only to be condemned in 1795 to pay Latude a considerable amount in damages. Latude died a wealthy man.

40. Hephaestion was one of Alexander the Great's generals. He and Alexander's friendship was sometimes compared to that of Patroclus and Achilles; Alexander was overcome with grief at Hephaestion's death, only eight months before his own. It is not entirely clear why Jacob mentions Hephaestion in this line.

41. Percinet is one of the two protagonists of "Graciosa and Percinet," a fairy tale by Madame d'Aulnoy. Percinet has the gift of fairy magic and repeatedly helps his chosen love, Graciosa, who is persecuted by her evil stepmother. His "beat" is presumably the duty of constantly protecting Graciosa.

42. Monsieur de Montserrat is presumably Joaquín de Montserrat (1700–1771), viceroy of New Spain from 1760 to 1766. Several disasters occurred during his term as viceroy. It is once more unclear why Jacob mentions this character here.

43. This *Poupon, roi des grenus*—literally "infant, king of the grainy ones"— seems to be Jacob's invention. A granita is an Italian confection made of ice whose texture is coarse and grainy.

44. *Gaster* (Greek for "stomach") is Rabelais's godlike incarnation of human appetites, responsible for humankind's greatest deeds and creations, and also for humankind's greatest atrocities; see *Gargantua*'s final chapters. But "Gaster" is also a German surname, and Jacob might have something else in mind. *Amanita* designates a genus of often poisonous mushrooms, including the entheogenic *Amanita muscaria*, which causes hallucinations of infamous potency.

45. I have opted to mention Chekhov's comic short story "The Darling" to maintain the rhyme, whereas Jacob mentions Sheridan—referring probably to satirical Irish-British playwright Richard Brinsley Sheridan, part of an entire family of writers (his mother Frances, a novelist; Thomas Sheridan, a proponent of classical oratory, and his sisters).

46. The word *baie* can mean either "berry" or "bay"; Jacob seems to be playing on the word's double meaning.

47. Peris are fairies or magical spirits featured in Persian folklore.

48. Balaam, an evildoing non-Israelite prophet, is sent to curse the Israelites; he blesses them instead, in Numbers 22. Belém is a populous northern Brazilian city whose name means "Bethlehem" in Portuguese. Jacob is likely riffing here on the Latin word for war: *bellum*. Brigadier Laramie: Jacques La Ramée (his name's spelling has many variants) was a fur trader from Quebec who explored Wyoming. Aramon is a variety of red wine grape.

49. Ovid was reportedly in exile among the Scythians; Delacroix painted several paintings called *Ovid Among the Scythians* (1859 and 1862).

50. Aeolus is the name of one of several mythological figures; his name is associated with the wind.

51. Aviatic: of or relating to aviation; the word is attested. Heligoland: a small archipelago in the North Sea inhabited by Frisians.

52. Dagestan is a small republic in the Caucasus. It joined the Soviet experiment in 1921.

53. An *aronde* is a piece of hardware called a dovetail, and is also an archaic word for "swallow" in French. I have opted to maintain the word for its sonority (and I suspect it is attested in English).

54. Nantes is a city at the southern edge of Brittany (its status as a Breton city has often been contested by other Bretons). Besides various other prisons, the Château of Nantes, a small fortress located in the center of the city, has often served as a prison.

55. Clisson is a town seventeen miles from Nantes.

56. Malachite is a deep green precious stone with beautiful patterning. Its name comes from the mallow plant.

57. The *almanach de Gotha* was a directory of Europe's nobility and royalty. The original directory was maintained and published annually until 1944.

58. Camphor has long been used to treat various forms of pain including coughing and sore throat, arthritis, hemorrhoids, and others. Phosphorous was first used in the eighteenth century to treat various fevers. Phosphorous has been used for abortion, and camphor is unsafe for pregnancy; could the dancer in question be pregnant?

59. Cuscuta is a mostly tropical and subtropical genus of parasitic plant whose various species are known by many names including strangle-weed, fireweed, or witch's hair.

60. Bhopal is a city in India. I chose this city for the rhyme; Jacob has "Vienna," but the sense is the same: the poet can't remember where this took place; it could have been anywhere, including the Southeastern French village of Draguignan.

61. Emir Abdelkader (1808–1883) was an Algerian leader who led an uprising against French colonial power in the nineteenth century. Abdelkader was also a scholar and religious figure. He has often been praised for his humanity.

62. Jacob has "Mademoiselle Biscorne," which could mean something like "Mademoiselle Twohorns," but the adjective *biscornu* means "distorted" or "deformed"; hence my "Miss Contort."

63. Bukhara is a very old city in Uzbekistan located on the Silk Road.

64. Jacques I Androuet du Cerceau (1510–1584), often known as Ducerceau, was a famous French architect and designer. He was not the architect of the Pont-Neuf, which predates him; it seems likely that Jacob is playing on the meaning of his name: a *cerceau* is a hoop or ring, evoking the cartwheel at the end of the verse.

65. Followers of Pelagius (ca. 354–418) believed in free will (as opposed to predestination) and the goodness of the human soul (as opposed to the wickedness suggested by the doctrine of original sin).

66. Jacob's syntax here is unclear; the verse lacks any discernable subject, and *faire un tour en bateau*, to "take a ride in a boat," only vaguely seems related to what the husband was asked. I have maintained the disjunctive logic of the original.

67. I've approximated the whimsical spelling of Jacob's imaginary street.

68. Claudio Castelucho y Diana (1870–1927) was a Catalonian painter who lived in Paris; Jacob, as a friend of Picasso, may have regarded Castelucho's painting as academic and retrograde. Gnome et Rhône was an early aircraft engine manufacturer; their planes were used by the French during World War I. Jacob spells the name of the company with an additional circumflex on the name Gnome (Gnôme); I have maintained his aberrant spelling.

69. *Le Déjeuner sur l'herbe*, which means "the lunch on the grass," is the famous painting by Manet.

70. The name may be Jacob's invention or a misspelling; there does not appear to be a place called Marcajola.

71. This appears to be a diminutive of the tenora, the instrument evoked in "Honor of the Sardana and the Tenora."

72. Jacob has *marche*, which can mean either "step" (as in a step on a set of stairs) or a "march" (as in a group of people marching). Since the verse is obscure, I have taken greater liberties here.

73. Theodosius I, called "Theodosius the Great," was Roman emperor from 379 to 395. He made Christianity the state religion, and undertook major architectural projects in Constantinople.

74. *Patois* can refer to any number of French regional dialects, some of which are very different from French, and most of which have been nearly persecuted out of existence in the last hundred and fifty years.

75. Alençon is a well-known variety of needle lace. Estérel is a volcanic range on the Mediterranean whose profile resembles lace; Jacob's verse specifies *le point d'Estérel*, which could be either "Estérel point," as in a mountainous point jutting out into the sea, or "Estérel stitch" by analogy with *le point d'Alençon*, another name for Alençon lace.

76. The "Triplex car . . . sides of the shaft" seems in part to be describing this very unusual pair of shoes.

77. Jean-Joseph Farina, inventor of cologne (the perfume), who changed his name to Jean-Marie Farina. Farina was the model for César Birotteau in Balzac's 1837 *Histoire de la Grandeur et de la Décadence de César Birotteau, marchand parfumeur* (see O., 1769, note 16).

78. A pari-mutuel, or parimutuel bet, is a form of wager wherein bets are pooled, and the pool is shared among winning bets, as in horseracing especially.

79. Pascal's wager is the famous passage in the *Pensées* which argues that rationally, we ought to believe in God, since if God does exist, we would go to Hell for not believing in Him, but if God does not exist, we lose nothing by believing in Him. Of course, this is assuming God does not reward those who don't believe in Him, and that God is benevolent.

80. Madapollam is a soft cotton textile, used for embroidery, handkerchiefs, and the like. Madapollam is also the name of a village in India, once the site of the cloth factory of the East India Company. Spanish White may refer to a white wine from Spain, an off-white color, or whiting used in paint or other construction-related substances.

81. To parge is to cover masonry, as for the creation of stucco.

82. Jacob's verse is enigmatic here, but might be a play on nonsense words used in French songs: "rataplan plan plan." "Rata" is also a common nickname for ratatouille. I also drew a blank in the translation of this verse.

83. The Grande Maison de Blanc was one of the *grands magasins*, a precursor to today's department stores. It is now a landmark of Art Nouveau architecture located in Brussels. The Samaritaine building in Paris was built for the same purpose in a similar style.

84. In this context, a culverin is a late-medieval ancestor of the cannon.

85. Georges-Édouard Lemarchand, known as Georges Dorival or simply Dorival (1871–1939), was a French actor, painter, and art collector. Well-known in the 1920s, he worked as a permanent member of the Comédie française troupe from 1917 until his death. He was a defender of Jacob's work, and indeed recited his poems at the Comédie française.

86. Maria Felicia Malibran was one of the nineteenth century's most famous opera singers, an archetypical diva who sang both contralto and soprano. She died at the age of twenty-eight, becoming legendary for her voice and dramatic personality.

87. A corregidor was a Spanish royal administrator and judicial authority from the fourteenth to the eighteenth century. The impasse de Guelma (thus named in 1877) is a street in Paris now known as the villa de Guelma (name changed in 1986). It is in the eighteenth arrondissement, in Montmartre, as is the rue Ravignan.

88. The rue Caulaincourt is another famous street in Montmartre.

89. A logogriph is a form of word-puzzle involving anagrams.

90. This is probably an allusion to the four years of World War I, 1914 to 1918.

91. Counterfactual: Jacob would practice astrology until his death.

92. The Four Crowned Martyrs whose names Jacob provides here died while refusing to sacrifice to the god Aesculapius. Their story is known among others by way of the *Golden Legend* of Jacobus de Varagine, a thirteenth-century compilation of saints' lives.

93. Barabbas is the insurgent Jew arrested at the same time as Jesus, who was freed in place of the latter (Mark 15:6–15 and elsewhere in the New Testament). Sesostris was a Pharaoh who Herodotus claimed made military incursions into Europe, particularly in Asia Minor. The Thracians were a tribal people who lived in the Balkans and Anatolia especially, and were described by ancient Greeks as warlike and barbarous.

94. Salvator Rosa (1615–1673) was an Italian mannerist painter whose brooding style has been seen as anticipating European Romanticism.

95. Liège is an important city in Belgium; the Bidasoa river is a French and Spanish river that flows through the Basque country.

96. Fortuné du Boisgobey was a popular French novelist who made his début with a series called *Lettres de Sicile* in 1843; Horace Lecoq de Boisbaudran was a French artist who taught Rodin among others. Jacob appears to be conflating the two, and neither were governors over the Kingdom of the Two Sicilies, but Jacob might have a third personage in mind.

97. A solfatara is a kind of fumarole or volcanic vent; there are many of these at the Phlegraean Fields, a volcanic area near Naples, which made up part of the Kingdom of the Two Sicilies. The Solfatara crater properly speaking lies at this volcanic site, and was once supposed to be the home of the god Vulcan.

98. Tartarus was supposed to be a very deep part of the underworld in Greek mythology, where great criminals and monsters roamed.

99. A steerage is the "coach" area of the boat, for passengers with the least expensive accommodations.

100. A screamer is a South American bird, one of three distinct species of crested duck-like water birds.

101. Foxgloves, or *digitalis*, are a deadly poisonous plant with long stalks lined with bell-shaped blossoms.

102. The rue Bourg-Tibourg lies in the Marais neighborhood of Paris, but Jacob's allusion remains obscure.

103. Perigal-Nohor is an entirely invented word, but it does vaguely evoke the names of certain famous gemstones, particularly the Koh-i-noor, and the word "noor," which could conceivably be mistranscribed *nohor* in French, means "light" in Farsi.

104. Saint Catherine, or Catherine of Alexandria, is a renowned virgin martyr whose historical details remain disputed. She is often represented holding a sword, and is the patron saint of students and schoolchildren, among other things.

105. Peter Abelard was a medieval scholar who had an affair with his student Héloïse d'Argenteuil, whose father castrated him by way of punishment. Seven letters between Héloïse and the then-renowned theologian and scholastic philosopher have survived along with the tale of their love.

106. See *supra*, note 103.

107. Napoleon named the first Duke of Otranto, the statesman and minister of police Joseph Fouché (1759–1820), in 1809.

108. Indeed, the city of Chatou does not have a castle.

109. There are many places called Montserrat, including a number of monasteries in Spain, a mountain in Catalonia, and an island in the Caribbean. The vagueness of the designation may well be deliberate on Jacob's part.

110. The rare verb *étrenner* means to wear or experience for the first time; I have translated it here as "to try."

111. An edema is a swelling caused by excess bodily fluid.

112. This name appears to have been invented by Jacob.

113. In Charles Perrault's version of "Bluebeard," Bluebeard's wife has a sister named Anne who is asked by the wife to climb the tower and watch for the arrival of the brothers so that they can save the wife from death at Bluebeard's hand. The brothers arrive in the nick of time. While Anne is watching for the brother, the wife calls up to her: "Anne, my sister, do you see anyone?"

114. These may well be actual folk-remedies of old.

115. Loaches are a bottom-dwelling freshwater fish often bearing a sucker-like mouth.

116. Auer lamps are generally known as Welsbach gas lamps or Welsbach burners in English, developed by Carl Auer von Welsbach in the nineteenth century, developer of the metal-filament lightbulb, among other discoveries and inventions. Jacob indeed writes "Auer ramp" rather than "Auer lamp."

117. Jacob might have Mignon's song from Goethe's *Wilhelm Meister* in mind; the refrain of this famous poem might be translated as "do you know . . . ?"

118. Acteon surprised the goddess Artemis (presumably the "Diana" mentioned later in the poem) while the latter was bathing; Artemis transformed Acteon into a hart and set his own dogs on him.

119. It is unclear why the sleet is Malagasy, if not for the rhyme between *malgache* (Malagasy) and *cache-cache*. I opted for a slant-rhyme here, translating *grêle* (hail) as "sleet."

120. A helot is a serf of ancient Sparta, with a status between that of a slave and that of a citizen.

121. Probably Giambattista Basile (1566–1632), courtier and Italian poet, and also a collector of fairy tales.

122. Triboulet was Nicolas Ferrial, the court jester of Louis XII and Francis I of France, and one of the most famous jesters of all. He appears in François Rabelais' *Third Book of Pantagruel* and in Victor Hugo's play *The King Has Fun* (*Le Roi s'amuse*), attesting to his legendary status.

123. Léon Gambetta (1838–1882), French politician, especially notable for his role during and after the Franco-Prussian War. He was unable to prevent a loss in that war, though he had originally opposed it as well as Napoleon III generally. Simón Bolívar (1783–1830) was a Venezuelan political and military leader who led what are now several South American countries to independence from the Spanish empire. He is a hero of independence in those countries.

124. An aerolith is another name for a meteorite. It is unclear what Bolívar's "tube" refers to.

125. See note 116.

126. Pierrot was originally a Commedia dell'Arte character who became the stock figure of French pantomime: pale white skin with a black skull cap or a pointed cap and a loose-fitting white costume. He is an ancestor of the classic English and American clown figure, but Pierrot is often a sad and melancholy figure (but funny as well, of course). Many Pierrots can be found in front of Notre Dame during tourist season.

127. Birthwort, though in fact toxic, was long thought to be useful for problems during labor, as its leaves resemble the shape of a uterus. Needless to say, a birthwort bouquet is a strange gift for the engaged young woman, and suggests she might already be pregnant (hence the signing of the papers in preparation for a wedding, not to mention the slightly suspicious presence of the sailor . . .).

128. See *infra* note 209.

129. I propose a reading of this apparently obscure poem in my article "Parlez-vous jacobien? Exégèse d'une traduction," *Cahiers Max Jacob*, no. 10 (2010): 75–87. This poem is in part a riff on lines by Paul Verlaine, including "Petits amis qui sûtes nous prouver . . ." from the collection *Sagesse*. Verlaine counts among Jacob's most important literary forefathers.

130. To be "mithridated" is to be rendered immune to a poison by taking small doses over a long period of time; the term comes from the story of Mithridates VI, "the Great," who attempted this. Jean Racine wrote a tragedy called *Mithridate* (1673) based on this monarch's story.

131. The peritoneum is the membrane encasing the internal organs of the abdomen.

132. This poem parodies a famous fable by La Fontaine, "The Crow and the Fox": in this fable, the crow has caught a piece of cheese; the fox flatters the crow for his beautiful singing voice; the crow opens his beak to sing, and the cheese falls to the ground, where the fox eats it; hence the analogy between crows and women, foxes and men in Jacob's poem.

133. The Pantheon is a French monument where many famous individuals (mostly men) are buried. It is considered a great honor for one's remains to be moved to the Pantheon, which is located in the fifth arrondissement of Paris.

134. Electra is the sister of Orestes, and assists him in avenging his father Agamemnon's murder at the hands of Aegisthus and Clytemnestra. Both Sophocles and Euripides wrote tragedies called *Electra*. Jacob's allusion remains, however, unclear.

135. Bellona was an ancient Roman goddess of war.

136. A spirit lamp is a small burner that uses alcohol as fuel.

137. The title may come from a forgotten popular tune.

138. Uranian is a late nineteenth-century term for a homosexual man. The term may also be astrological, referring to anything connected to the planet Uranus.

139. John Chrysostom denounced the lavish and decadent lifestyle of Aelia Eudoxia, empress by marriage to the Roman Emperor Arcadius. This line appears to assume the attitude of Chrysostom confronting the Empress.

140. Averroes, or Ibn Rushd, was an Andalusian philosopher. He was partly responsible for reintroducing Western Europe to Aristotle's thought, hence his potentially heroic status here.

141. In Molière's *School for Women*, the ridiculous Arnolphe says to Agnes: "il est aux enfers des chaudières bouillantes, / Où l'on plonge à jamais les femmes mal vivantes" (there are in hell boiling furnaces / where they dunk forever women who live badly). But Arnolphe is trying to frighten Agnes into submission through sneaky moralizing. Jacob may be mocking his own poem's apparent admonitions by way of the allusion to Molière.

142. Nitre is potassium nitrate, or saltpeter, used notably for making fertilizer and gunpowder. It can be manufactured from some organic materials such as guano (hence, perhaps, Jacob's connection of nitre to one's "backside").

143. Mortadella is a kind of sausage resembling bologna with white spots.

144. Senna is an herb used as a laxative and to treat certain digestive problems.

145. Ceruse is white lead, a poisonous white pigment derived from lead carbonate and lead hydroxide, once used for paint as well as for the sixteenth-century whitening cosmetic called Venetian ceruse.

146. Catherine Monvoisin (1640–1680), known as La Voisin, was an alleged sorceress, a fortune teller, and an infamous poisoner tied to

Parisian aristocracy under the reign of Louis xiv. After the "poison affair" implicating several prominent aristocrats, thirty-six people were executed. Madame de Montespan was La Voisin's most famous and important client, and the mistress of Louis xiv. Montespan allegedly arranged a Black Mass through La Voisin, and employed her for witchcraft. After the poison affair, Montespan's credibility and influence were seriously damaged.

147. A bottine is a lady's small boot.

148. The Boulevard Malesherbes is a wide, long boulevard of the eighth arrondissement that leads to the church of the Madeleine, built by Napoleon I. Napoleon III inaugurated this boulevard in 1861; it was part of the Baron Haussmann's urban planning projects of the nineteenth century. The "triumphant return" could refer to either Napoleon, perhaps, though the first Napoleon's triumphant return from the Island of Elba before his defeat at Waterloo some hundred days later is probably the famous incident alluded to here.

149. A portmanteau word combining *Villon* and *villanelle*. François Villon was a famous *mauvais garçon* (bad boy) of the fifteenth century, and a major poet of that era responsible for the "Ballade des dames du temps jadis," with the refrain usually translated as "Where are the snows of yesteryear?" A villanelle has five tercets and one quatrain, only two rhymes, and two refrains. This poem is, of course, not a villanelle, but its historical allusions resemble Villon's ballads.

150. Tripolitania was a former province of Libya, and included the city of Tripoli. In 1921, Tripolitania was a republic (it dissolved in 1923, and Italy would take control of the region from 1927 to 1934 under Mussolini).

151. Zeuxis was a legendary painter of ancient Greece. An ancient anecdote claims that birds pecked at grapes he had painted; he was noted for his realism.

152. "Well, let me think" is how I have translated *Qu'il m'en souvienne*, but the expression is ambiguous, since it seems to express a desire ("I wish I could remember") but suggests an ironic delivery ("I can't be bothered to remember" or a disingenuous "I can't recall"). It could also mean something like "I'd better try to remember, or else." There might be a half-dozen interpretations of this expression in this poem.

153. Figuière was the publishing house of Eugène Figuière, and a major force in publishing in the early years of the twentieth century.

154. An apocrisiary was a kind of medieval diplomat something like an apostolic nuncio; the title was used by Byzantine ecclesiastical ambassadors, among others. The idea is that of a cleric who acts as the ambassador of an ecclesiastical authority in the secular world.

155. Jacob refers to how they paint in China; I have altered this for the sake of the rhyme.

156. The "crooks" here are the hooked sticks of the shepherds mentioned in line four. Grésivaudan is a valley of the French Alps where Grenoble is located, a likely site for shepherds.

157. Chios is the fifth-largest Greek island in the Aegean Sea. Tenedos is a Turkish island of that sea.

158. A pioupiou is a term for a soldier, but also sonically evokes a little bird.

159. A marabout is a Muslim holy man or hermit.

160. A wherry is a kind of rowboat. Jacob mentions *péniches*, more like a kind of light barge.

161. This line may refer to Alain (1868–1951), the pseudonym of Emile-Auguste Chartier, a French philosopher and pacifist. His brand of political moralism has been largely forgotten.

162. Jacob mentions Barèges, a town in Southwestern France, and Baume-les-Dames, a town in Burgundy. I felt that Indian names with similar sonorities and rhythms might be more evocative for Anglophone readers.

163. Ipecac is a vomit-inducing drug, and was once used to purge the stomach of poisons.

164. Limpopo is the northernmost province of South Africa, and is named for the river Limpopo. The Congo is also a river.

165. Max Jacob's brother-in-law was Lucien Lévy (1876–1942), married to Jacob's favorite younger sister Mirté Léa. Robert was their son, who was severely intellectually disabled, and lived for much of his life in an assisted care facility. Lucien Lévy was a jeweler by trade.

166. An epitome is a miniaturized summary that ostensibly encapsulates the essence of a longer work.

167. Francis Thomé (1850–1909), a French pianist and composer known for several operas and operettas as well as salon music.

168. See note 165.

169. An aubade, from the word *aube* (dawn), is a kind of song or poem sung by the lover when leaving at dawn after a lover's tryst.

170. The mazurka is a Polish musical form that is danced to, in a lively, often triple tempo. The varsoviana, on the other hand, is a slow, graceful dance.

171. Lahore is the capital of the Punjab province of Pakistan.

172. Royat and Mont-Dore are towns in the Auvergne region of central France. This region is considered quite remote wilderness by French standards.

173. No sultana of this name seems to be attested.

174. An obsolete term for primates, i.e., mammals with four limbs and opposable thumbs.

175. *Pleurer comme une Madeleine* in French means to weep a great deal, presumably in reference to the repentant Mary Magdalene.

176. Jacob is playing on the word *esprit*, which means "spirit" in several senses. The *esprit nouveau* designated the poetic avant-garde of the late 1910s and early '20s; the term may have been coined by Guillaume Apollinaire.

177. Calf's head or *tête de veau* is a popular French specialty, but is made all over Europe. A *tête de veau* can also be an insult to designate an idiotic person, not unlike "shit for brains."

178. The allusion remains obscure, and this name may be Jacob's invention. It has the flavor of a stage name.

179. Georges Gabory was a young writer friend of Jacob's who frequented the office of the anarchist-leaning journal *Action*, run by Florent Fels between 1919 and 1922. Gabory wrote often for that journal, and also prefaced the abridged edition of Jacob's *Dice Cup* that Fels published in 1922 through the publishing house Stock.

180. This company appears to be Jacob's invention, though it vaguely evokes the names of circus acts or fairground troupes. Here, it evidently designates the company that ran the old bazaar.

181. The *méridienne* mentioned by Jacob is a daytime nap or a kind of couch, while the *meridien*, also mentioned, is the same as the English "meridian"—the concept used in acupuncture, or the imaginary geographical boundary line. Jacob seems to have every meaning of these terms in mind.

182. "Invitation to a Voyage" is also the name of one of Charles Baudelaire's most famous poems. The resemblance basically ends there, as Baudelaire's piece is a delicate love poem, while Jacob's poem meditates on technological modernity.

183. Louis Bergerot was a friend of Jacob's as early as 1901. He was an employee at the Gare de l'Est.

184. Panhard was a French motor vehicle manufacturer, and one of the first makers of automobiles. Panhard et Levassor was originally established in 1887, and Raymond Poincaré adopted a Panhard vehicle as the first presidential automobile.

185. See *infra*, note 216.

186. Dvorak might be a kind of liquor. Byrrh is a quinine-based wine aperitif developed in 1866, and especially popular in the early twentieth century.

187. The Pigalle neighborhood in Paris has long been a favored location for prostitution.

188. America's name comes from that of Amerigo Vespucci, not from Columbus.

189. Bartolomé de las Casas (1484–1566) was a Spanish landowner who became a Dominican friar after arriving in Hispaniola. He documented the colonial atrocities committed in the early years of settlement in the Caribbean.

190. Pedro Álvares Cabral, a Portuguese nobleman and military man generously considered the first European explorer to discover Brazil, in 1500, just a few years after Columbus's well-known landfall in the "West Indies" in 1492.

191. Pamiers is a town in the Southwestern corner of France, in Occitania. Vervins is a town in the North of France. Pont-Aven is a Breton village known for having attracted many painters. The meaning seems to be: the correspondence might come from any corner of France, or indeed from anywhere at all.

192. Castalia is the name of several American cities, in Iowa and North Carolina.

193. Jacques-Charles-Louis Clinchamps de Malfilâtre (1732–1767) is an underappreciated French poet sometimes compared to his contemporary Nicolas Gilbert.

194. Jena Bridge (the Pont d'Iéna) is one of the bridges over the Seine, now linking the Trocadéro neighborhood to the Eiffel Tower. It was built by Napoleon to commemorate his victory at Jena.

195. In the French as in my English, the syntax is particularly tortuous here; "they" in line 2 designates the buffets that "beguile" the "rabble," while at the same time, those buffets "abhor the kisses" of the same "rabble" (which designates the partygoers in disguise). The buffets appear to express their abhorrence in "telegraphic style," a possible allusion to the blinking of the crystal atop them. This elaborate game of layered metaphors and self-reflection is eminently Mallarméan in spite of the comic elements involved.

196. Scapin is the French version of Scapino, a character of the Commedia dell'Arte characterized by his constant fleeing from one thought or situation to another—he is always attempting to *escape*. *Les Fourberies de Scapin* is a famous farce by Molière.

197. Eurotas was a mythological king of Laconia associated with the origins of Sparta; it is also the name of a river. Guastalla is an Italian city. The implication seems to be that some of the guests are dressed as geographical locations. Since Acteon had no known children, it seems the guests dressed as "Acteon" and "Fantasia" have several children.

198. Sosie is a servant of the king Amphitryon. In Plautus's *Amphitryon*, adapted later in versions by Molière and Kleist, Mercury impersonates Sosie, and the two meet (Mercury wins). The common noun *sosie* in French refers to a doppelgänger.

199. Leander, of the mythological story of Hero and Leander. Daphnis, mythological shepherd and inventor of pastoral poetry.

200. Dorimène is a name recalling those of classical theatre, particularly Molière; Monsieur Jourdain, in the *Bourgeois gentilhomme*, courts a widowed marquise named Dorimène.

201. There is more than one Aristarchus, but Aristarchus of Samothrace was an ancient grammarian. An "aristarch" refers to a severe and nit-picky critic, by reference to this grammarian.

202. For the sake of sonority, I commit a small anachronism here: lycra, the substance that makes up Spandex, was not invented until 1958.

203. Probably André Masséna, a military commander of the French Revolutionary Wars as well as under Napoleon, nicknamed "the dear child of Victory." To find Louis XV's tailor and Masséna in the same space might seem incongruous.

204. *Coppélia* was an 1870 comic ballet based on E. T. A. Hoffmann's famous story "The Sandman," in which a young man falls in love with an automaton called Coppelia. The story is not comic at all, being one of the masterpieces of the eerie fantastic.

205. Jacob does not use a comma, but "a hot abscess" indeed appears in apposition to the "crowd."

206. Benares is a city on the Ganges in India, and a major religious site (hence the minarets, presumably). Epirus is a region in Southeastern Europe.

207. Calabria is a region of Southern Italy known for licorice, citrus, and many other agricultural products, among other things.

208. The battle of Salamis was fought between Greece and Persia in the fifth century BCE. Themistocles led the Greeks to victory against Xerxes, though the former were outnumbered.

209. Matamore is a famous braggart; he is the ridiculous Capitan of the Commedia dell'Arte, full of empty bluster, but a *matamore* can designate any braggart in French. Marsupio (Marsupiau, in Jacob's spelling) evokes a character from the Commedia dell'Arte, though he appears to be Jacob's invention.

210. Mignonette is another name for reseda. "Virgil" appears to be used as an adjective here, as in "Virgilian."

211. Pamplona is the capital of Navarre, part of the Basque country in Spain. The choice appears motivated by the rhyme in this instance.

212. Contrary to appearances, this poem is not autobiographical: the last line of the French version refers to the brother as the "eldest brother," but Jacob was not the eldest brother of his family. He may have in mind another family member, or the whole might be considered an allegory for internal conflict.

213. The name Malvina was popularized by the Scottish writer James Macpherson, responsible for the *The Poems of Ossian*. It is also the title of an opera by Nicola Vaccai (1816). Jacob was likely familiar with both Vaccai's opera and the *The Poems of Ossian*, though it is unclear what role they play in this poem: the name seems designed to evoke a certain kind of theater, specifically the melodrama.

214. *Mikado* was once the Japanese term for the emperor; it is now considered obsolete.

215. The dog-rose or *Rosa canina* is a species of wild rose. It is a climbing shrub.

216. Synagoga and Ecclesia, the synagogue and the church, are allegorical figures adorning many Catholic places of worship; Synagoga is typically represented with a blindfold. This poem dates from 1907, having first appeared under the title "Scène d'intérieur" in the *Dernier Cahier de Mécislas Golberg*. Golberg and his close friend Jean-René Aubert were among the first to publish Jacob's poetry. The early date suggests that titles or notes like "Written in 1903" may well not be fictional.

217. The *cnemis* is the shin area.

218. Diagoras of Melos was a fifth-century atheist philosopher. Xenophanes of Colophon was one of the most important presocratic philosophers and a polytheistic theologian of ancient Greece.

219. The "Calabrian Joachim" is no doubte Joachim of Fiore, born in Calabria (*circa* 1135–1202). He founded the Abbey of Fiore there. It's unclear what the "book of popes" refers to; Joachim was the author of influential apocalyptic texts of the Middle Ages, and was sometimes touted as a sort of prophet (hence his connection to Nostradamus here). "Centuries" refer to Nostradamus ten-line groups of verses in his *Prophecies*.

220. Mount Ararat is the biblical resting place of Noah's ark. It now names a province and dormant volcano in Armenia.

221. The Bois de Boulogne seems to be conflated with "countryside" in these lines (slightly modified in translation), but the Bois is a large park at the southwestern edge of Paris, and is extremely domesticated for "countryside." Proust dedicates many celebrated pages to the Bois de Boulogne.

222. Charenton was an infamous insane asylum, the French equivalent of Bedlam.

223. Manuel Ortiz de Zárate was a minor modernist painter born in Italy to Spanish parents, and raised in Chile. He knew Jacob in Paris, where he lived during the cubist years and during World War I. According to Jacob's reports, Zárate, like Delaw mentioned below, experienced visions of divinity around the same time Jacob did, in 1909.

224. Georges Delaw was a celebrated turn-of-the-century illustrator who published in many newspapers of the period. He lived near Jacob in Montmartre around 1909. See previous note.

225. Amalek was a great enemy of the Israelites, and chief of the Amalekites. In this context, "the Amalekite" means something like "the Enemy."

226. The name Micomusa appears to be Jacob's invention.

227. Quatre-Temps probably designates another shopping location like the Bon Marché department store already mentioned; the Westfield Les Quatre Temps of today, for example, is a giant mall at La Défense, to the immediate West of Paris.

228. The quai de Grenelle is a road on the Seine in the fifteenth arrondissement of Paris (left bank).

229. Charles-Maurice de Talleyrand-Périgord, known as the Prince of Talleyrand, was a clergyman and diplomat who represented the Catholic church to the French crown; his career spanned from the reign of Louis XVI to Louis-Philippe, through the Revolution and the Napoleonic empire. His name, in this context, stands for great glory and power.

230. Gaspard II de Coligny was a Huguenot leader who favored a diplomatic approach before being murdered during the Saint Bartholomew's Day massacre, when many Huguenots were killed. This reignited the major conflicts of France's wars of religion between Catholics and Protestants.

231. Louis IX of France notably built the Sainte Chapelle in Paris, Saint Louis's personal chapel. Louis was a major patron of the arts, and promoted gothic architecture.

232. I.e., denying the existence of God, insofar as it is a form of blasphemy, presupposes a form of belief in God.

233. Moloch was a Canaanite god, not a Papuan god: Jacob is speaking figuratively; i.e., the Papuans worship primitive and/or abhorrent idols. Moloch is notably associated with human sacrifice.

234. The cubist painter Juan Gris and Max Jacob were especially close during the 1910s. In 1921, Gris would illustrate a story by Jacob published by Daniel-Henry Kahnweiler's Galerie Simon under the title *Ne coupez pas Mademoiselle ou les erreurs des PTT*.

235. The Brocken is the highest mountain in the Harz mountain range, in Northern Germany.

236. The year 1793 was the year of the Terror, when anti-antirevolutionary repression reached its height; some 3,000 people were guillotined that year by the revolutionary government.

237. This verse, with slight variation, also occurs in "Nocturne."

238. The Trocadero Palace, built in 1878 in a neo-Byzantine style, was dismantled in 1935 and replaced by the Palais de Chaillot in 1937.